To Kill a Mockingbird

A Summary of Harper Lee's Classic Novel

Trisha Lively

To Kill a Mockingbird 100 page summaries

Printed in the United States of America.

ISBN: 978-1-939370-03-7

Library of Congress Cataloging-in-Publication Data

Lively, Trisha
To Kill a Mockingbird A Summary of Harper Lee's Classic Novel/
Trisha Lively

Table of Contents

Short Summary

Harper Lee's *To Kill a Mockingbird* recounts a few pivotal years in the young life of Jean Louise "Scout" Finch. It is set in the Depression-era small town of Maycomb, Alabama and begins in the summer when Scout was five years of age. Scout, her nine-year-old brother, Jem, and their six-year-old friend, Dill, who visits his aunt in Maycomb every summer, engage in spirited, frolicsome play-acting and fantasy-driven diversion. The children become fixated on a mysterious, reclusive neighbor, Arthur "Boo" Radley, who never leaves his house and whose past, as they hear from the town gossips, is riddled with scandal. At once frightened by and obsessed with Boo, the children craft elaborate schemes to make contact with him, much to the chagrin of their widowed father, Atticus, a respected lawyer in Maycomb, who implores the children to respect the Radley family's privacy. After two summers of intrigue, Boo Radley begins leaving gifts for the children, though they are unsure whether the gifts are coming from him.

Scout and Jem's fantasy play world is soon interrupted by the harsh reality of racial prejudice. Atticus is assigned as the defense attorney for a black man, Tom Robinson, who is charged with raping a white woman. Many town residents already consider Tom guilty because of the color of his skin, and reproach Atticus for his attempt to mount a real defense for his client. Soon Scout and Jem are also subjected to the town's wrath as they are taunted by neighbors and classmates because of their father's actions. Scout initially gets into fistfights to defend her father and family, but Atticus makes her promise to ignore her tormentors' remarks and to exercise restraint. Atticus himself is confronted by an angry mob and the conflict is defused only by the unexpected intervention of Scout, Jem and Dill. By exposing the children to the town's deep-seated racism, the trial becomes a learning experience for them as they discover that many of their neighbors, friends and even teachers hold opinions and beliefs that differ starkly from their own.

Though Atticus forbids his children from attending the trial, they, along with their friend Dill, sneak into the observation balcony reserved for blacks. They hear the testimony of the alleged victim's father, Robert Ewell, the town drunk, and of the alleged victim herself, Mayella Ewell. When both witnesses are cross-examined by Atticus and when Tom Robinson takes the stand, it becomes clear that he did not rape Mayella but that Mayella had made a sexual advance toward him and suffered a beating at the hands of her father when he caught her in this act. Atticus also brings to light a physical ailment Tom suffers which would have made it impossible for him to beat and rape Mayella, as she claims. While the jury exits to deliberate on the case, Jem expresses his confidence that Tom will be exonerated, citing the overwhelming evidence that shows his innocence. When the jury returns with a guilty verdict, Jem is disillusioned and Scout and Dill are left confused over the seemingly contradictory actions of many of the adults in their community. Though Atticus is confident that Tom stands a good chance of being cleared on appeal, Tom's doubt in legal justice for blacks leads him to an ill-fated escape attempt from prison. He is shot to death by guards while scaling the prison fence.

In the months following Tom's death, the emotions that ran high during the trial begin to settle as routine life in the small town resumes. Robert Ewell, however, is disgraced and consumed with resentment toward those involved in the case. He spits in Atticus's face in the center of town, he breaks into Judge John Taylor's house, and he hounds and intimidates Tom Robinson's widow. On a dark Halloween night, Ewell attacks Scout and Jem while they are returning from a school pageant. He slices open Scout's costume with a knife and breaks Jem's arm before a mysterious man intervenes and rescues the children, carrying the unconscious Jem home to his father.

The town's sheriff soon discovers that Robert Ewell is dead as a result of knife wounds, and Scout comes to understand that her rescuer is none other than Boo Radley, whom she meets for the first time in her injured brother's room. Atticus assumes Jem killed Robert Ewell in self-defense, though it is unclear whether Jem or Boo stabbed him. The law-abiding Atticus begins contemplating the legal proceedings that must take place, but the Sheriff believes holding either Jem or the painfully shy Boo responsible for the murder would be unethical and insists that Robert Ewell fell on his own knife. Atticus eventually yields to accepting this version of events.

Scout accompanies Boo home, where he re-enters never to be seen again. While standing on the Radley house porch, Scout looks at her neighborhood anew from Boo's perspective and laments the opportunity she missed of thanking him for the gifts.

CHAPTER 1

What happens?

The story begins with the narrator's recollection of her brother Jem's broken arm when he was thirteen years old. As we shall see, this is where the story ends as well. Before recounting the events that led to the injury, the narrator gives a history of the Finch family in Alabama and of its estate, Finch's Landing. The family lost its wealth during the Civil War, but descendents continued the tradition of living on what the land at Finch's Landing produced. The narrator's father and uncle broke this custom when the former left to study law in the state capital of Montgomery and eventually settled in the town of Maycomb (twenty miles from Finch's Landing), and the latter went to study medicine in Boston. Only the narrator's aunt and her taciturn husband remained at the Landing.

Following the family profile, the narrator turns to a description of Maycomb, where she grew up living with her widowed father, her older brother and the family housekeeper and cook, Calpurnia. The children's mother died when the narrator was only two years old. Maycomb is depicted as a slow, sleepy place where people meander with no particular destination and where the summer heat paralyzes everyone.

The plot begins in the summer when the narrator was five going on six. Though it is not yet revealed, the narrator's name is Scout. Summer is just starting, and she and her nine-year-old brother Jem engage in their routine play in the yard. They soon discover a young boy hiding in the collard patch of their neighbor Miss Rachel Haverford's garden. He introduces himself as Charles Baker Harris, though everyone calls him Dill. Dill announces that he can read, even though he is only six years old, and that he lives in Meridian, Mississippi with his mother, though he does not know his father. The children become fast friends and spend the summer enacting scenes from their favorite books.

Eventually, they turn their attention to the mysterious Radley family house and its most notorious resident, Arthur "Boo" Radley. Jem tells Dill the story of Boo, who got into trouble as a teenager and has been locked inside his house ever since. Scout adds that several years later Boo stabbed his father in the leg with a pair of scissors and spent a few nights in the county jail. Though no one has seen him for years, rumors fly about Boo lurking through the neighborhood at night. Dill's interest in Boo continues to grow, and he dares Jem to touch the Radley door. Though Jem hesitates at first, he builds up his courage and does it and then runs, without turning back, to the safety of his own yard.

Analysis:

This chapter lays the foundation for the entire novel as it depicts the southern mindset, the static setting of Maycomb, and a child's perspective on the world. There are clear-cut and fixed social rules in Maycomb, and success and acceptance in this society are dictated by these rules. In an indirect and seemingly unwitting way, Lee's narrator describes Maycomb in a manner that captures the oppressive nature of the conventions and traditions that govern the town's social order.

This is evident from the outset in the narrator's profile of the Finch family history. Heritage and lineage are important factors in defining a family's place in Maycomb's social ranks, and though the Finch clan no longer has money, it has a long history in the territory, a history that solidifies the position of its current descendants as an established and respectable Maycomb family.

That the unwritten social rules are rigid and immutable is also conveyed through the narrator's description of Maycomb itself as a static place where no one has anywhere to go or much of anything to do. Routine defines the town's life, and digression from it is generally frowned upon. The town's inhabitants also fit into neat categories, the most predominant division being between Maycomb's whites and blacks. The character of Calpurnia helps establish this division as we see blacks in a service role to the white community and we are familiarized with the expectation of their quiet acceptance of this rank when Scout expresses surprise over Calpurnia's criticism of Mr. Radley because she, "Rarely commented on the ways of white people."

At this early stage, the children accept Maycomb's conventions uncritically, not yet recognizing a need to question them; however, some of their characteristics already reveal them as dynamic figures operating in this static setting. For one, Scout is a tomboy and shuns the convention of dressing or behaving like a girl. Second, Dill is somewhat of an outsider, coming from Mississippi, though he has relatives in Maycomb. These lively, diverse features foreshadow the personal evolution and growth the children will experience, and they define this novel as a coming-of-age story (*Bildungsroman*).

But their progress will occur gradually. For now, the children are part of Maycomb's inert fabric as evidenced by their superstition (an extension of the town's indulgent superstition) concerning Boo Radley. Engrossed by the mystery of his existence, they allow their vivid imaginations to determine their opinion of Boo and of the Radley family in general. The only figure challenging this way of thinking is Atticus, the family's and, eventually, the town's voice of reason.

That the children are poised to commence a personal journey is made evident by the chapter's end when Jem accepts Dill's dare to touch the Radley house. Here we see that facing life's challenges, no matter how small or insignificant, requires courage, and Jem and his companions possess this trait.

Key takeaways:

It is important to recognize the narrator's point of view as the story is told in retrospect by the adult Scout many years after the events took place. Despite the passage of time, the narrator recounts the story from a child's perspective and with a child's understanding (or lack of understanding). The interpretation of events can often be unsophisticated or left up to the reader to consider from an adult, experienced point of view. Only on a few occasions does the narrator interject a mature commentary, and it is usually done to advance the story.

The town of Maycomb is almost a character in itself. Indeed, Lee's description of it in this chapter is similar to the way she develops the novel's protagonists. Perhaps one of the narrator's most suggestive remarks is that "A day was twenty-four hours long but seemed longer." The town's plodding pace is captured in this quote, which renders life as at a virtual standstill.

Lee is particularly adept at depicting life through a child's eye. Consider Jem and Scout's boundaries at this point. They could go as far as "Mrs. Henry Lafayette Dubose's house two doors to the north of us, and the Radley place three doors to the south. We were never tempted to break [these boundaries]." At a young age, children's lives exist partially in their physical surroundings and partially in the fantasy world of their minds. Lee understands the children's acceptance of these physical limits and their lack of intention to exceed them at this point.

Language is a very important aspect of the novel, especially with regard to race. In this first chapter, the narrator uses the term "Negro" to describe African Americans. As we will see, the narrator as well as other characters use the more explosive term "nigger." While this word is particularly offensive to our contemporary sensibilities, its use in the novel is powerful, especially as we see Scout learn not to use it.

CHAPTER 2

What happens?

At summer's end, Dill returns to Mississippi, while Jem and Scout prepare for the new school year, which will be Scout's first. Her experience of school is not positive. Many of her classmates are repeating the first grade, and the new teacher, Miss Caroline Fisher, is displeased when she learns that Scout (here we discover that her real name is Jean Louise) already knows how to read and write in cursive. Miss Fisher insists that reading ought to be taught by a licensed teacher only and that cursive writing should not be learned until the third grade.

When lunchtime arrives, Scout finds herself in more trouble. Miss Fisher, who is from northern Alabama, which for the children is nearly akin to being an alien, does not understand Maycomb's customs and habits. Upon discovering that Walter Cunningham Jr. did not bring a lunch, she cannot understand why he will not accept a quarter from her to buy his lunch and which he can pay back the next day. Scout explains that Walter, "Is a Cunningham," a point that is perfectly clear to her and the other students, but lost on Miss Fisher. To clarify further, Scout tells Miss Fisher that she is shaming Walter by offering him money because the Cunninghams survive on what they have and do not accept handouts or money they know they cannot repay. Taken aback by Scout's straightforward manner, Miss Fisher scolds her by slapping her hand with a ruler and making her stand in the corner, a punishment to which the class responds with great laughter.

Analysis:

The issue of class comes to the forefront in this chapter as Scout, the daughter of an educated lawyer and state legislator, is in school alongside farm kids and children who are repeating the first grade, some not for the first time. Through the narrator's description of the town's children, the reader comes to see the many layers of Maycomb's white adult society. The strongest contrast is between the confident, precocious Scout, who personifies her father's learned ways, and the quiet, hesitant though polite Walter Cunningham Jr., who embodies his father's hard-working, accept-no-charity farm ethic.

This chapter also further emphasizes Maycomb's conventions and customs as it shows the difficulty an outsider, Miss Fisher, has in decoding them. Scout's explanation that Walter won't accept a quarter because he is a Cunningham makes no sense to the new teacher, who requires further elaboration to understand the situation. Her encounter with someone who does not understand the town's ways compels Scout to recognize a limit in her worldview and adjust to someone who needs help understanding Maycomb and its inhabitants.

The interaction in this chapter between Scout and Miss Fisher also highlights another of the novel's themes: convention vs. reason. Rather than praise Scout for her ability to read and write in cursive, Miss Fisher scolds her for the sole reason that Scout's skills do not adhere to the school's prescribed pedagogical sequence. Miss Fisher cannot see beyond the rules she learned in her teacher training to recognize the admirable talents of a young first grader. Rather, she encourages her young pupil to stop learning on her first day of school.

That Scout knows how to read and write singles her out and separates her from the rest of her schoolmates. Again we see that the novel's young protagonist is dynamic and not easily wedged into society's fixed categories. It is already possible to detect a future clash between the Finch children, who have animated, active minds, and Maycomb's stagnant society, which is averse to change and diversity.

Takeaways:

In describing northern Alabama, where Miss Fisher is from, the narrator refers to the region as full of, among other things, "Big Mules." This is a term used to describe powerful figures that exert strong political and economic influence especially by controlling either individuals or their votes. It is doubtful that the young Scout would have understood the meaning of this term. Rather, she was likely parroting what she heard from the adults in her community.

When Jem inquires of Scout how her first day of school is going, Scout responds spiritedly: "Jem, that damn lady said that Atticus's been teaching me to read and for him to stop it." This is the first time we hear Scout using bad language, another un-lady-like habit of hers, which grows worse before it gets better. We also see her referring to her father by his first name—more evidence that not only Scout, but her family is unlike the rest of Maycomb. Atticus allows his children to refer to him by his name because he respects them as individuals and treats them similar to how he treats adults. This bending of the rules at home contributes to shaping Jem and Scout's unique qualities.

Lee captures a child's naiveté when she has Jem explain to Scout that Miss Fisher is a proponent of the Dewey Decimal System. Jem is confused because he has heard that Miss Fisher adheres to the progressive education theories of John Dewey. But when he tries to explain this to Scout, he mistakenly refers to her pedagogical style as the Dewey Decimal System, which is a library classification system developed by Melvil Dewey in 1876, not a theory on education.

CHAPTER 3

What happens?

While the class is exiting the school for lunch, Scout jumps on Walter Cunningham in the yard and begins beating him up until Jem intervenes. Scout explains that Walter had caused her to get off on the wrong foot with the new teacher (this scene is the first time that the narrator is called by her nickname, Scout). Jem calms Scout and invites Walter home for lunch.

Atticus engages Walter in conversation about farming matters, which puts the nervous child at ease. When Walter asks for syrup and proceeds to pour it all over his food, Scout embarrasses him about ruining his meal. Called to the kitchen by Calpurnia, Scout is scolded and told to eat in the kitchen if she cannot treat her guests kindly.

Back at school, Miss Fisher shrieks upon seeing a bug fly out of Burris Ewell's hair and orders him home to bathe before returning to school the next day. Burris informs Miss Fisher that he has no intention of returning, and the other children must bring her up to speed on another Maycomb custom: the Ewell kids only ever attend the first day of school to keep the truant officer at bay. Distraught by the numerous mishaps of her first day teaching, Miss Fisher bursts into tears, but is soon comforted by her students.

At home in the evening, Atticus asks Scout to read with him, but she uses the opportunity to convince him that she does not need school. She recounts her challenging day to Atticus, who asks her to consider the situation from Miss Fisher's point of view, for she is new to both Maycomb and her job. Atticus offers Scout a compromise: they will continue reading together each evening, despite Miss Fisher's admonitions, if she will agree to go to school.

Analysis:

Though Scout is a unique figure who defies conventional labeling, she is also a child who has a lot to learn, as this chapter illustrates. Her attack of Walter exposes Scout's impulsive side and her ridiculing of him during lunch shows that, while she might know Maycomb's customs, she does not yet understand the importance of social graces. If she follows the model set by Atticus, however, Scout will mature into a thoughtful, compassionate adult. This chapter showcases Atticus's kindness and forethought. Comprehending Walter's apprehension about joining the family for lunch, Atticus puts the child at ease by talking to him about the few things he knows: farming and hunting.

In the evening, Atticus teaches the art of compromise to Scout as he convinces her to continue with school. By requesting that she keep their agreement a secret, Atticus also introduces Scout to an adult concept: the well-intentioned untruth. Unlike most fathers, Atticus treats his children with the same respect he shows adults, and trusts they will comprehend the advanced ideas he exposes to them. The secret Scout will now keep from her teacher seems unimportant in comparison with the main lesson Atticus imparts to his daughter in this conversation. After listening to Scout's version of the day's events, he asks her to see things from Miss Fisher's perspective, thus highlighting one of the novel's central themes: empathy.

Atticus's calm and thoughtful behavior toward his children as well as Walter foreshadows the role (a sort of father-figure role) he will come to play in the town during Tom Robinson's trial. His measured, deliberate comportment earns him the town's respect, even from those who disagree with his decision to defend Tom.

Takeaways:

For Scout, school is the first time she is exposed to a disciplinary model and to authority figures outside of her family. Though her experience is not positive initially, it is evident that she is merely experiencing the necessary growing pains of someone leaving the safe familial cocoon and entering broader society. This transition is good for her as it opens her world to new experiences and challenges, and it forces her to grow. This theme of evolving from comfort (or innocence) to complexity recurs throughout the novel. Indeed, Scout's transition to school is easy in comparison with the complex realities she will encounter as the plot unfolds.

This chapter also brings to light another unconventional aspect of the Finch family: namely, the role of Calpurnia as surrogate mother and unofficial family member. When Scout embarrasses Walter for pouring syrup over his meal, Cal calls her to the kitchen, scolds her and teaches her how to treat guests, and Atticus fully expects Cal to do this. In society, a black person would not scold a white person, even with a difference of age. But in the Finch household, those rules do not apply as Cal is respected and cherished.

In this chapter, the reader gets a first glimpse of the Ewell family, represented by the grubby Burris Ewell who leaves school and his new teacher in tears. Introducing one of the Ewells, Lee further develops the many layers of Maycomb's white society as the Ewells fit into a unique category: degraded and disrespectful outcasts, quite unlike both the educated Finches and the polite, hard-working Cunninghams. In her naiveté, Scout does not yet recognize the difference between herself and Burris Ewell, and uses his choice not to attend school as an example of why she should not be forced to go to school. As the story unfolds, the young protagonist sees more clearly how unpleasant the Ewell family actually is.

CHAPTER 4

What happens?

Scout eventually settles into the routine of school and her troubles begin to fade away. Walking home one day, she notices something shining in a knothole of a tree in the Radleys' yard and grabs it to find two pieces of chewing gum in tinfoil. At home, Scout tries the gum and is pleased to find it is not poisoned (town rumors sustain that everything from the Radley yard is lethal). When Jem returns, he forces her to spit out the gum and to gargle. On the last day of school, Jem and Scout see more tinfoil in the same knothole and discover a jewelry box with two Indian head pennies. They are unsure whether they have discovered someone's hiding place or whether someone is leaving these gifts for them.

Dill soon arrives from Mississippi, and the children resume the play-acting they had mastered the summer before. Bored by the usual stories, they begin discussing "Hot Steams," which Jem explains to be ghosts stuck on Earth because they cannot enter Heaven. They finally resolve to play with an old tire, and Jem launches Scout, who has climbed into the tire, down the street. Veering off course, the tire with Scout in it bumps into the Radley house porch. Jem runs to rescue his sister and the tire.

Following this incident, Jem devises a new game: acting out the Radley family lives. As summer progresses, the children grow ever more involved in the game until Atticus discovers them in the yard acting out the story of Boo stabbing his father's leg with scissors. Atticus disproves of their game, and Scout begins to grow weary of it as well.

Analysis:

While she devotes two chapters to Scout's first day of school, Lee then passes over the rest of the school year in a few lines, suggesting that Scout's real education takes place outside the classroom. Indeed, with the gifts left in the knothole of the Radley tree, Scout is being taught a lesson in kindness, though she remains unaware of this for a long time to come. Neither she nor her brother can fathom that Boo Radley, the town oddity and nutcase, could be responsible for such acts of kindheartedness. Their minds are not open yet to seeing Boo differently from the identity the town has foisted upon him. Jem will not even let Scout enjoy the gum she found on the Radley family property.

Despite their fear of Boo, the children's obsession with him grows, fuelled in large part by Jem, who conceives of the game of acting out scenes of the mysterious family's life. While their play-acting is callous, as they will come to realize later in the novel, it becomes a tool for Jem to display his bravery, as he is not scared to act out the life of Boo, the subject of many of his fears, and he continues to do so even after his father forbids it. As in the first chapter, Jem's courage is blossoming, though perhaps not in the way it should.

Key takeaways:

Lee again depicts the white and black societies of Maycomb as two separate spheres. In response to Jem's description of Hot Steams, Scout tells Dill not to believe him, citing Calpurnia who says, "That's nigger talk." Implicit in this remark is the notion the blacks and whites have two distinct understandings of the world, the former's version being more superstitious than the latter's. The irony, however (an irony that the young Scout does not seem to grasp), is that this criticism of blacks' belief in superstition is uttered by a black character. The further irony is that while irrational beliefs are attributed to blacks, they are readily evident among the white community as well.

Interestingly, the term "nigger" comes to mark Scout's progression of thought and awareness. In the novel's early chapters, she uses it when she is parroting or repeating what others have said and does not seem to comprehend the word's weight. As Maycomb's prejudices become evident to her, however, especially when her father's role as Tom Robinson's lawyer exposes her to teasing, Scout begins to recognize the word's odious connotations.

While Lee highlights again Jem's growing courage, she also balances it against his more childlike notions, such as superstition. Jem encourages Dill's interest in mystery with his fanciful story about the Hot Steams, which even includes a mantra that protects from these Steams. As he matures in the novel, Jem later recalls this story and laughs at himself for taking it so seriously—a sign that he is leaving childhood fantasies behind him.

CHAPTER 5

What happens?

Scout manages to dissuade Jem from playing the Radley family game. The result is that Jem and Dill spend more time together and neglect Scout, even though Dill had only recently proposed marriage to her. Scout passes the extra time with Miss Maudie Atkinson, who lives across the street. Miss Maudie is kind to the kids and, importantly, does not interfere in their lives. She maintains a beautiful garden and is known for her wonderful cakes, which she bakes often for the children.

During her visits with Miss Maudie, Scout ascertains more information about the Radley family. Boo's father, Mr. Radley, was a strict Baptist, and the family lived according to a severe religious doctrine. As Miss Maudie puts it, they "Are so busy worrying about the next world, they've never learned to live in this one." Scout wonders whether Boo is crazy, to which Miss Maudie replies that if he wasn't before being locked up, he certainly is now.

When Scout rejoins the boys, she discovers they have been plotting to make contact with Boo by using a fishing pole to put a note through one of the Radley house's windows. The plan does not unfold as expected: Jem's fishing pole is not long enough to reach the window, and Dill fails in his role as lookout, as Atticus catches Jem in the act of attempting to pass the note to Boo. Atticus orders the children to leave Boo alone and to respect his privacy. He also forbids them from playing the Radley family game.

Analysis:

Excluded by the boys, Scout gradually edges into the female world with her visits to Miss Maudie. Her kind neighbor represents not only an open-mindedness akin to

Atticus's, but also an acceptable version of femininity for Scout. It is ironic that while the boys are off indulging their fantasies about Boo, Scout is actually collecting evidence that broadens her understanding of his reclusiveness and provides a larger familial context in which to consider his odd behavior. This marks the beginning of a shift in Scout's attitude about Boo. As we shall see, she eventually begins to fear him less and pity him more.

She has not, however, made that transition to empathy yet, as she agrees to go along with the boys' plan to make contact with him. Though distasteful, the boys' scheme shows that their interest in Boo is also shifting away from fear of him to a more genuine curiosity about him as a person. They want to know what he does and how he lives. Despite this mild shift in their intentions, their interest in Boo is still an obsession, and Atticus is the only figure who manages to temper it, at least temporarily. Exhibiting uncommon tolerance, Atticus instructs the children to leave the Radley family alone, emphasizing that they are doing no wrong to anyone. Unlike many people of Maycomb, Atticus does not fear the Radleys, but understands that they choose to live their lives in a different manner from all the others. Though Atticus's advice is important, it does not sink in with the children until later in the novel when they begin to understand why someone might wish to withdraw from society.

Key takeaways:

It is useful to see Miss Maudie's garden as a symbol of her open-mindedness, for, unlike practically everyone else, she actually loved the weeds "And everything that grew in God's earth ... With one exception . . . one spring of nut grass could ruin a whole yard." Symbolically, the Ewell family constitutes the nut grass, as their actions, which are based on ignorance and prejudice, throw the town into turmoil and bring its ugly divisions to light.

While a great deal of the novel seeks to dispel assumptions about blacks, it also devotes some attention to blurring the distinction between the male and female spheres. Conventionally, men are seen as occupying the terrain of reason, while women are generally considered more emotional. Scout's effort to extract reliable background information on Boo Radley seems highly reasonable, however, especially in contrast with Jem and Dill's silly plan to pass a note through a window using a fishing pole. In this way, she becomes a younger version of Atticus as the voice of reason among the kids, though it is a role she is unaware of occupying.

It is interesting that the children do not seem to comprehend Atticus's inclination to treat the Radleys normally. When he is berating the kids for their attempt to contact Boo, he reminds them that the civil way to communicate with someone is by knocking on the door, not slipping a note through the window. Jem, Dill and Scout's impression of Boo as a mysterious outsider prevents them from treating him with common kindness and civility. He is still not humanized in their eyes.

CHAPTER 6

What happens?

Despite Atticus's warning, the boys' interest in Boo continues to grow. On the night before Dill's return to Mississippi, the children head out for a walk, though Scout soon discovers their intentions to look inside one of the windows of the Radley house. Scout agrees to go along with the plan only after her complaining prompts Jem to accuse her of being a girl. The children slide under a wire fence behind the house and maneuver their way through the garden and past a squeaky gate. While Jem is on the porch looking through the window, Scout sees the shadow of a man approaching him, raising its hands and then turning away. Frightened, the children rush through the garden toward the wire fence when they hear a gunshot. They quickly squirm under the fence, but Jem's pants get caught on the wire and Scout has to return to help him pull them off.

The neighbors are gathered outside the Radley house, and they inform the children that Mr. Radley was shooting at a "Negro" in his yard. When everyone notices that Jem is not wearing pants, Dill quickly comes to his rescue, claiming they had been playing strip poker. Atticus instructs Jem to get his pants back.

Scout lies awake in the middle of the night fearing Boo when she hears Jem moving about. He has decided to retrieve his pants because he does not want to upset Atticus with the truth of how he lost them. Scout waits in fear for Jem to return, expecting to hear another shotgun blast, but is relieved when he returns with his pants.

Analysis:

Even though the children's interest in Boo might be more genuine than it was at the novel's beginning, their intention is still to gawk at him, not to establish a friendship. Their prejudices about him, which are based on the town's gossip, prevent them from seeing him as a potential friend—only as an eccentric. Their narrow-mindedness is symbolic of the town's prejudices toward blacks, who are treated as outcasts and despised for their perceived differences. Indeed, Mr. Nathan Radley's immediate assumption is that a "Negro" was prowling around his yard, an assumption accepted unquestioningly by most of the neighborhood.

With this scene, Lee develops another recurring theme: the deception of appearances. No one in the neighborhood (except Atticus, as it will later be revealed) would imagine three white children roaming through the Radley yard late at night. This was the sort of deceiving, immoral behavior many considered innate among blacks. Knowing the truth probably would have shocked many people, especially the gossipy Miss Stephanie Crawford who wholeheartedly accepts the story that a black man was prowling around. Of course, the children themselves are also deceived by appearances with regard to Boo, as they remain convinced of his strangeness.

It seems somewhat odd that in the midst of these scenes that highlight the children's misconception of Boo, Lee chose to showcase Jem's bravery. Out of fear of losing his father's respect, Jem wanders out into the night to retrieve his pants, returning to the very site where he was shot at earlier. The risk involved in this endeavor was outweighed by his dread of disappointing Atticus. Lee's depiction of Jem captures the sometimes confused moral development of youth who occasionally follow the right path, but just as often veer off course.

Key takeaways:

When Scout discourages the boys from executing their plan, Jem accuses her of "Acting like a girl," a slight Scout can hardly bear. Ironically, though, it's the girl who is offering the wisest advice in the situation and who sees how their plan could have grave results. Overcome by their obsession to know more about Boo, the boys don't heed Scout's warnings and carry on. They would have been much better off, however, if they had "Acted like girls."

In this chapter, the use of the term "nigger" begins to distinguish characters from one another. When the children approach the neighbors gathered in the Radley yard after hearing the shotgun, Miss Maudie explains that, "Mr. Radley shot at a Negro in the collard patch," using the more socially acceptable way of referring to blacks. Miss Stephanie Crawford follows on this, claiming that Mr. Radley "Says that if anyone sees a white nigger around, that's the one." While Miss Stephanie may have been merely repeating Mr. Radley's words, her use of the "N" word seems gratuitous nevertheless—and not wholly surprising as she has already been depicted as a shallow figure. As the novel progresses, the use of this term exposes the divisions in Maycomb's society.

This chapter also contains the book's only reference to kudzu, a large-leaf and quick-growing vine common throughout the American South.

CHAPTER 7

What happens?

For a week following Jem's late night excursion to retrieve his pants, he is distant and cranky. The children begin another school year, and after the first week, Jem finally tells Scout what has been disturbing him. When he snuck out to recover his pants, he found them folded neatly on top of the fence and discovered that the tear in them had been sewn up, though in a untidy manner, "Not like a lady" would have sewn them.

Passing by the knothole one day, Jem and Scout discover a ball of twine in it, though Jem refuses to take it, thinking the hole must be someone's hiding place. After a few days, however, when he sees the twine still there, Jem resolves to take it and any other items left in the hole. After some months, he discovers two dolls carved out of soap lying in the hole. Scout dislikes the dolls because they resemble her and her brother, but Jem is fascinated by them. Over the following weeks, the children discover more gifts in the hole, including a pack of gum, a medal from a spelling bee and a broken pocket watch. Jem and Scout resolve to leave a thank-you note in the hole, but when they return to it, they find it filled with cement.

Jem asks Nathan Radley if he had placed the cement in the hole, which he affirms, claiming that the tree is sick. Jem seeks Atticus's opinion on the tree, and he proclaims it looks healthy to him. On the porch that evening, Scout thinks Jem may have been crying.

Analysis:

This chapter marks an important transition in Jem's thinking about Boo, for the recluse's kind gestures toward Jem finally humanize him in the boy's eyes and elicit genuine feelings of friendship in him. Jem is unable to process this feeling at first, as the discovery of his mended pants folded neatly merely confuses him. But with time and a succession of thoughtful gifts, Jem begins to see Boo in a new light, one that is unclouded by prejudice or bias. For the first time, he seeks to treat his peculiar neighbor civilly by writing a thank-you note for the gifts.

That Jem is thwarted in his effort to express gratitude to Boo is important as it symbolizes the obstacles one can face when one's thinking or actions go against the conventional grain. In some ways, Jem's effort to thank Boo is similar to Atticus's attempt to defend Tom Robinson: both seek to do what is right, but encounter hostility from those afraid of change. In Jem's case it is Nathan Radley who cuts him off from Boo, presumably because Nathan intends to maintain his brother's isolation from the world.

When Jem realizes he missed his chance to thank Boo, he cries—a conventionally female response to a situation and not a behavior usually associated with manliness. However, Jem's emotions, rather than undermining his masculinity, seem to reinforce it, as they show he is maturing, leaving behind childhood fantasies and misconceptions and readying himself to see the world anew. He understands that Nathan Radley is being cruel to Boo, and he laments the injustice of it. Jem will have a similar response to Tom Robinson's trial. The process of growing up and grasping the complexities of the adult sphere will be painful and disillusioning for Jem, as he will learn some very unsettling truths about his community.

It is important to note that Jem's emotional development from this point forward accelerates, while Scout advances at a more gradual pace. The siblings' differences now become ever more evident.

Key takeaways:

Jem's concern over the cement in the tree is important, for he believes he knows that Nathan Radley is lying about the tree being sick. Determined to find out the truth, he asks Atticus's opinion, which is that the tree looks healthy. Jem is forced to digest the idea that an adult is lying to him and also cutting him off from Boo. It is one of many harsh realizations Jem will reach over the course of the novel as he himself advances toward adulthood.

While Jem's ideas about Boo may be evolving, his understanding of gender roles seems fixed, as evident in his remark that his pants were not mended neatly, "Not like a lady" would sew. This attitude that sewing is women's work would have been common in 1930s America, as very few men would have been adept at the skill. It is this division of labor and the division of spheres that Scout has trouble accepting, for her inclinations do not necessarily coincide with society's expectations for females.

When Scout first sees the soap dolls Boo carved for them, her reaction was typically feminine: she yelled in fear, dropped them and thought about "Hoodoo," or a person or thing that causes bad luck. Jem, on the other hand, reasons that someone must have watched them closely in order to render the two of them so well. As he reflects on who could have produced them, it is implied that he realizes it is Boo. Scout does not make the same connection.

CHAPTER 8

What happens?

Winter sets in, and the children hear one of their neighbors, Mr. Avery, lament how bad children bring about changes in the seasons. One morning Scout awakes to an unknown sight: an unusual winter storm has dropped snow on Maycomb, and the children enjoy a day of play in the white powder as school is canceled. After collecting all the snow they could from Miss Maudie's yard, the children build a snowman by constructing it first in mud and then covering the figure in snow and designing it with a distinct likeness of Mr. Avery. Though amused, Atticus makes them change it.

Atticus wakes the children in the middle of the night, urging them to get dressed and go outside as Miss Maudie's house has caught on fire. Atticus leaves the children in front of the Radley house and rushes to help the neighbors put out the blaze. Once everything is under control, the kids return home, where Atticus notices that Scout is wrapped in a blanket not belonging to them. They cannot figure out who has placed the blanket around Scout. Jem uses the opportunity to tell Atticus all about the knothole and his pants. Atticus finally points out to Scout that it was likely Boo who brought her the blanket, and she is frightened by the thought of having been so close to him. The next day it is resolved that Miss Maudie is to stay with Miss Stephanie Crawford until her house is rebuilt.

Analysis:

The symbolism of snow and fire is important in this chapter. On the one hand, the snow could represent the death of Jem's childhood, as he embarks on a new path to adulthood. It could also stand for the peace or serenity reached between the children and Boo through the receipt of his gifts, which elicits their sympathy for him. Finally, the snow could symbolize the calm before the storm, as the children enjoy one final episode of spirited, mischievous and childlike play in a pure, untainted snow-white setting before society's ugly truths are foisted upon them.

This last interpretation is reinforced by the middle-of-the-night fire that abruptly ends the day's joy with a violent surge of pain and suffering. Lee is foreshadowing the emotional jolt the children will experience as a result of Tom Robinson's trial. The author does not allow the fire to completely dampen spirits and extinguish hope, however. In the face of calamity, the neighbors join together to fight the blaze, exemplifying the idea of community and fellowship. And Miss Maudie herself manifests optimism the morning after as she cheerfully shares her plans to build a smaller house and a larger garden. Thus, even as danger (and later injustice and prejudice) threatens the small town, goodwill and care for others overcome despair.

Key takeaways:

In this chapter, Lee uses the figure of Mr. Avery as a tool to represent superstitious, uncritical thinking in adults. When the cold weather comes, he blames the change of seasons on bad children and frightens Jem and Scout with his interpretation. With this unfeeling, mythical comment, Mr. Avery represents the elements of Maycomb society who rely on tradition and convention rather than reason as a basis for their behavior and decisions. The town will soon see the danger these elements present.

The novel's gothic atmospherics are clear in this chapter, with the drama of the late-night fire and the mysterious (missed) appearance of Boo Radley. Though Boo's kind gesture toward Scout further humanizes him, his stealthy manner contributes to his mystifying aura, building up the suspense of one day meeting him in the flesh.

In addition to maturing, Jem also increasingly solidifies his relationship with Atticus, as evinced by his confession to this father about the knothole and his mended pants. As he navigates his path to adulthood, Jem clearly sees the value of honesty.

CHAPTER 9

What happens?

Scout's world soon goes from lovely snow to fire, just as Miss Maudie's house had. Hearing Cecil Jacobs say that her father defends "Niggers," Scout is infuriated and she readies herself for a fight with her young schoolmate. At home, she asks Atticus about Cecil's remarks. After instructing her not to say "Nigger," he explains the case of Tom Robinson and his role in defending him. Atticus tells Scout that many people in Maycomb don't want him to mount an actual defense for Tom, but he feels a moral obligation to do so and would not be able to respect himself or expect his children to respect him if he did what people were pressuring him to do rather than what is right. He asks Scout to behave similarly by avoiding fights and ignoring the nasty remarks others direct at her. In response to Scout's question about whether he will win the case, Atticus utters a resounding no, but explains that it is important to try. His talk gets through to Scout who, the following day, walks away from another fight with Cecil.

Christmastime arrives and with it comes a visit from Jem and Scout's beloved Uncle Jack, who turns up with two long packages. Uncle Jack is surprised to hear Scout using bad language. On Christmas day, Scout and Jem open Uncle Jack's gifts to find air rifles, which they love. The family heads to Finch's Landing to celebrate the holiday with Aunt Alexandra and the children's cousin, Francis. The fun and feast are interrupted when Scout pounces on her cousin after he calls Atticus a "Nigger-lover" who is "Ruinin' the family." Uncle Jack pulls Scout off her cousin and punishes her. At home that evening, Scout tells Uncle Jack that he was unfair with her since he did not listen to her side of the story, which Atticus always does. When he hears what Francis said, he wants to go back and punish him, but Scout has him promise not to tell Atticus the reason for the fight.

Overhearing a conversation between Atticus and Jack, Scout is pleased to find that her uncle keeps his promise to her. She also hears Atticus commenting on the danger of her hotheadedness since things will only get worse as the trial nears. Atticus admits to Jack that he knows the jury will find Tom guilty, but he hopes to win on appeal. He wants to help his children get through this difficult period without catching "Maycomb's usual disease" of going "Stark raving mad when anything involving a Negro comes up."

Analysis:

The innocence of childhood is dealt a serious blow in this chapter, which pivots the story from the first plot, which focuses on a child's world of play, fantasy and superstitions, to the second plot, the very adult subject of Tom Robinson's rape case. The loss-of-innocence theme and the intrusion of mature matters upon youthful purity become ever more pronounced from this point forward.

Scout suffers confusion over how her family, which she believed lived in harmony with the community, could now become the object of ridicule. Her initial impulse is to defend her family with physical force, a youthful response which is tempered only by Atticus's discussion of his moral duty to defend Tom and his plea to her to exercise restraint. While various elements of Maycomb society are exposing Scout to the vicious aspects of the adult world, Atticus supplies her with its more positive features: ethical awareness, honesty, self-control and self-respect.

Compounding Scout's frustration over her family being negatively targeted is the concern over her lack of femininity expressed by Aunt Alexandra who now comes to figure in the story. Alexandra represents an extreme version of southern womanhood—one Scout has difficulty relating to. Her critical view of Scout exacerbates the child's feeling of sudden exclusion from society. When her beloved Uncle Jack then unfairly punishes only her for fighting with Francis, Scout is now the victim of injustice as well as of social ostracism. Lee partially resolves the child's suffering by redeeming Uncle Jack, who, upon hearing the truth, regrets his treatment of Scout, allowing her to enjoy some justice in the matter. And by keeping his promise to her, Uncle Jack also serves as a model of fidelity, which reassures the anguished Scout. This chapter vividly illustrates how growing up and entering the adult world can be an emotional roller coaster ride for a child.

Key takeaways:

When Atticus states, "Don't say nigger, Scout. It's common," he provides his daughter with a categorical condemnation of that offensive slur. Whereas before, she used the term in a relatively innocent and unknowing way, merely echoing the phrases she picked up from the adults in her life, she now has no excuse to continue uttering it, as she has been made aware of both its vileness and its power to harm.

Lee showcases Atticus's perseverance in this chapter. Though he knows he will not win the trial (maybe the appeal), he continues the fight, giving his all. The lesson is clear: certain defeat does not excuse someone from the moral duty of doing what is right.

In a similar vein, the predominance of ignorant behavior does not legitimize it. Atticus is determined to help his children avoid catching "Maycomb's usual disease" of prejudice toward blacks. Though he recognizes its pervasive and oppressive presence in the town, he refuses to allow his children to succumb to it merely because it's everywhere.

The meting out of injustice on innocents is a recurring theme in the novel, embodied most powerfully in Tom Robinson. This chapter also depicts Dill as an innocent victim who is scorned and dismissed by Francis because he lacks a stable family life. Making a child answerable or guilty for the situation he is born into and had nothing to do with creating is an injustice indeed.

CHAPTER 10

What happens?

The chapter opens with Jem and Scout lamenting their father's advanced age, complaining that he can't play football or other physical things that other fathers do. He even refuses to teach them to shoot their new guns. When Uncle Jack promises to teach them, Atticus tells Jem that, while he can shoot all the blue jays he wants, "It's a sin to kill a mockingbird."

Scout complains to Miss Maudie about how old the neighbors are and how Atticus can't do anything exiting. Even Calpurnia fails to come up with examples of Atticus's talents when questioned by Scout.

Off in the woods one day with their air rifles, Scout and Jem see Tim Johnson, a dog belonging to Harry Johnson, which is acting strangely. When they ask Calpurnia to have a look at him, she immediately determines that the dog is mad and calls Atticus in town. A few minutes later, Atticus and Sheriff Tate arrive with a rifle to shoot the dog. Sheriff Tate begins to take aim, but feels uneasy about making the shot and insists that Atticus shoots instead. Atticus heads to the middle of the street, aims the rifle and kills the dog in one shot. Scout and Jem are amazed by this feat, and as the neighbors emerge from their homes once the danger is gone, they learn that Atticus was once known as "One-Shot" Finch. Miss Maudie explains that he gave up hunting because his shot was so precise that it gave him an unfair advantage over the animals.

Scout immediately proclaims her desire to brag about Atticus's unknown talent, but Jem discourages her, saying he wouldn't like that. The chapter ends with Jem declaring how he doesn't care if Atticus can do nothing because he "Is a gentleman, just like me!"

Analysis:

In this chapter, Lee lionizes Atticus so that his children see, prior to the drama of the trial that is about to unfold, their father's courage and quiet dignity. Here again the theme of appearances deceiving resurfaces, as the children's view of Atticus as old and boring is shattered once they witness his bravery and sharp shooting eye, and learn of his previous glory as the town's best shot. Importantly, Jem does not draw inspiration from his father's shooting proficiency, but singles out his gentleman-like behavior—modesty, self control—as worthy of imitation. In Atticus, Lee offers readers an alternative to the traditional hero, who is admired usually for his physical strength and abilities. Atticus's heroic qualities consist of restraint, reserve, humility and decency.

The novel's main theme concerning the injustice of inflicting harm on innocents is given solid acknowledgement in this chapter as Atticus reveals the meaning of the work's cryptic title when he warns Jem that "It's a sin to kill a mockingbird." Mockingbirds do nothing but bring pleasure with their singing and thus to kill them is unjustifiable. This explanation recalls Atticus's reasoning concerning the Radleys, whom he thought should be left in peace as they do no wrong to anyone, and it foreshadows the tragic case of Tom Robinson.

Key takeaways:

It is possible to consider the mad dog as a symbol of the town. The children recognize that he is acting strangely, but he does not display the typical characteristics of a mad dog and he appears in February, an unusual time for a dog to suffer this condition. Similarly, the town appears normal and customary to the children until the extraordinary event of the trial reveals Maycomb's dark and dangerous underbelly.

The mad dog can also be likened to Tom Robinson. Not only are their names similar (the dog is called Tim Johnson), but so are their fates. Tim Johnson is killed after Sheriff Tate instructs Atticus to "Get him before he runs." Tom Robinson will be killed in an attempt to escape from prison.

That Atticus is the town's best shot is of course another symbolic feature of this chapter. Unlike many of his fellow townspeople, Atticus's vision is clear, allowing him to see right and wrong with no obstructions. Since he also has courage to accompany his visual sense, he becomes the town's protector, not only from mad dogs but from the town's own cruelty. Until this point, Lee depicts Atticus as an excellent father to his children; he will now become Maycomb's father figure.

CHAPTER 11

What happens?

Scout and Jem begin to turn their attention away from the Radley house and toward the other end of the street, which leads into town. Any journey in this direction, however, takes them past the house of Mrs. Henry Lafayette Dubose, a cantankerous old widow who insults them each time they walk by. On his way home from work, Atticus always greets Mrs. Dubose kindly and makes small talk with her.

Following Jem's twelfth birthday, Scout heads with him to town to buy a gift for him and a baton for her. As usual, Mrs. Dubose begins abusing the children as they pass by, particularly angering Jem when her insults focus on Atticus and his defense of Tom Robinson. As the children head home, Mrs. Dubose is no longer on the porch. Stopping in front of her house, Jem loses his temper and uses Scout's new baton to destroy her camellias.

When Atticus returns home from work, he sends Jem to apologize. While Jem is gone, Scout complains to Atticus about all the abuse they receive because of his involvement with Tom Robinson. Atticus hopes they will one day come to understand the reason he is putting the family through this pain.

Jem returns, explaining that he has apologized to Mrs. Dubose and has cleaned up her yard. He also reports that she wants him to come six afternoons a week for one month to read to her. Scout accompanies him on these visits, and the two are surprised by the fits she has, with her body shaking and mouth agape. Each reading session ends when a bell rings and the nurse appears to give Mrs. Dubose her medicine.

One evening Scout asks Atticus what a "Nigger-lover" is, to which Atticus responds that it is a term used by "Ignorant, trashy people" when they think someone is favoring blacks.

Jem and Scout come to realize that their sessions with Mrs. Dubose are lasting longer each day. When Jem's month ends, Mrs. Dubose asks him to stay another week, which Atticus forces him to do. In this final week, no alarm clock ever rings; rather, the children leave when Mrs. Dubose dismisses them, which is usually quite late and the reading sessions come to an end. Some months later, Mrs. Dubose passes away, and Atticus reveals to the children that she was a morphine addict who wanted to break her habit before dying. Jem's reading was a tool for her to keep her mind off the drug for longer periods each day until the habit was finally beat. Atticus encourages his children to see Mrs. Dubose as courageous, as she fought for something even though she knew she probably wouldn't win. In the end, however, Mrs. Dubose prevails and dies free of her addiction.

Analysis:

For Lee, the story of Mrs. Dubose becomes another way to present an alternative idea of courage. This weak, sharp-tongued, racist old lady hardly fits the typical ideal of a courageous hero, but Lee uses her fight against morphine addiction to illustrate the theme of true bravery, which is fighting a battle even when defeat seems certain. Like Atticus's defense of Tom Robinson, Mrs. Dubose is determined to battle her addiction because she believes it is the right thing to do. She does not want to die beholden to a drug, but free of her dependence and thus on her own terms.

Mrs. Dubose's situation and Atticus's admiration of her represent some of the many complexities of life, especially the baffling idea that good and evil can coexist in a person. For Atticus, it is important to see good in people and to believe that despite some evil behaviors, most people have the capacity and will to be good. This is how he thinks of

Maycomb, even as many townspeople hurl insults at him and his family. The coexistence of good and evil proves to be too sophisticated a notion for Jem and Scout, evidenced by the former's harsh reaction to the camellia Mrs. Dubose left for him.

Key takeaways:

Scout's inquiry to Atticus about the meaning of "Nigger-lover" illustrates her childlike innocence. She attacked her cousin for using the term even though she did not understand its meaning. Her anger about it signals that Scout now comprehends the "N" word's negative power and the adverse effects its use can have, for she is offended by it even though she is not black herself.

While Scout is not maturing at the same pace as Jem (and cannot be expected to do so), we do catch a glimpse of her development when she inadvertently reveals to Atticus the reason she attacked her cousin. She does not tell this to her father in order to justify her actions, but merely to seek clarification about the meaning of her cousin's slur. This shows that Scout is indeed exercising restraint.

CHAPTER 12

What happens?

Summer approaches and Scout is anticipating Dill's arrival. She misses him keenly because Jem has been distant and moody with her. Scout does not understand that Jem is growing up and experiencing puberty. Much to her dismay, she receives a letter from Dill saying he won't be coming to Maycomb this summer, but will spend time with his mother and her new husband. Atticus gets called away to a two-week session of the state legislature and leaves the children in Calpurnia's care.

Cal takes the children to her church, the First Purchase Church, on Sunday, and meticulously prepares them and their clothing in order that both appear well cared for. Everyone greets Jem and Scout kindly, except for one member of the congregation, Lula, who objects to bringing white children to an African-American church. The crowd stifles Lula and welcomes Jem and Scout to the church. Reverend Sykes begins the service by welcoming them both, and then Calpurnia's son, Zeebo, leads the congregation in a hymn by reading the lyrics aloud to everyone, after which they sing the words back to him—a practice that confounds Jem and Scout.

Another surprise is Reverend Sykes' sermon during which he actually names people in the congregation who have been sinning. He then demands that a total of ten dollars is donated to help Helen Robinson, Tom's wife, and locks the church's doors until the amount is obtained.

Raising this money for Helen Robinson prompts Scout to ask Calpurnia about Helen and about the accusations waged against Tom. Jem's curiosity is focused on the strange way the congregation sang the hymns. Calpurnia explains that most people there can't read so Zeebo reads it to them so they know what to sing. The children also show a greater interest in learning about Calpurnia's life and apprehend many details about her family and community during their walk home. For the first time, Scout is beginning to consider that Cal has a life beyond the cooking and caretaking she does for the Finch family and expresses a desire to visit Cal at her home one day. When the trio arrives home, they find Aunt Alexandra waiting for them on the porch.

Analysis:

The children's world is broadening, and this chapter takes them into Maycomb's black community. That they accompany Calpurnia without hesitation is evidence of their innocence as they see nothing wrong with the idea and are ignorant of the bad some townspeople might see in their associating with blacks. How the service unfolds—it differs in important ways from what Jem and Scout are used to—is a lesson in open-mindedness, for tolerant people understand that there is more than one way to do something. For Jem and Scout specifically, this opportunity to have first-hand experience of the black sphere humanizes the black community for them. Blacks are not abstract, silent or background figures in their lives, but real human beings, such as Calpurnia, about whom they care deeply, and Reverend Sykes, who is welcoming and warm to them.

It is important that this visit to Cal's church stimulates Scout to want to learn more about her dear housekeeper. Lee is illustrating how Scout's opinion of blacks will develop from her experience with them, not from the town's prevailing and uncritical prejudices. As any reasonable person would do, Scout and Jem judge people based on their behavior. This is the sort of thinking Scout applies to the Ewells in this chapter when she claims, "Well, if everybody in Maycomb knows what kind of folks the Ewells are they'd be glad to hire Helen." According to this logic, since everyone knows from experience that the Ewells are bad people, no one should heed their opinion on matters. What Scout does not comprehend, however, is how race trumps this logic.

Key takeaways:

Scout finds Jem's distance from her and his moodiness challenging, and she does not understand that it is attributable to puberty. But since they live together and she admires her brother, she is forced to tolerate his behavior and thus learns an important lesson in fellowship: patience and acceptance.

Like the Finch family, which is unique in many ways, Calpurnia stands out in the black community. She reads and speaks in a different manner, which the children notice once she begins to speak in the tone common among blacks. Her ability to empathize with others and to blend in with the community is very similar to Atticus's comportment. This chapter positions Calpurnia as one of the novel's role models.

Lee is not so naïve as to represent the black community as harmonious and free of discord. The character of Lula serves to illustrate that evil and prejudice are pervasive and exist even among those who suffer discrimination at the hands of others. That Lula is the exception rather than the rule, however, is Lee's way of comforting the reader and emphasizing the good in people.

CHAPTER 13

What happens?

Scout and Jem learn that Aunt Alexandra has come to live with them as a "feminine influence" for Scout. Alexandra immediately sets about organizing her social calendar and begins meetings with many different women, though she believes them inferior to her own family. Jem and Scout are soon exposed to Aunt Alexandra's obsession with heredity, as she attempts to instill in them a sense of pride in their lineage. Scout also gets drawn into Aunt Alexandra's social gatherings and is obliged every now and then to sit in on the usual tea. Alexandra seems to exercise some influence over Atticus, as she manages to get him to speak with Jem and Scout about the family's importance in the county. The conversation, which is so different from their usual chats with Atticus, falls flat and even upsets the children since they have never heard Atticus speak in this way. Sensing their unease, he tells them to disregard what he has said.

Analysis:

If their experience at Calpurnia's church broadened Jem and Scout's world, the arrival of their Aunt Alexandra threatens to diminish it as she brings the town's assumptions, conventions and prejudices straight into their living room. Her lessons on family heritage and social order fall on deaf, or at least confused, ears. Jem and Scout have not been raised to consider one's family history a defining element of their character. Living according to good principles and doing what is right are the components of good character. That Alexandra's message seems so foreign to the children reveals how far from the mainstream Atticus is and how strong his parenting skills are, even though he stumbles a bit when he agrees to discuss the Finch lineage with the children.

It is no accident that Lee highlights the stark contrasts between Maycomb's black and white worlds on the eve of Tom Robinson's trial. This structure builds up the anticipation of how these spheres will collide in the town courthouse.

Key takeaways:

Alexandra's discussion of Cousin Joshua reveals that she is cherry-picking moments from the family's history in order to remember only the good or socially useful aspects. When Jem innocently divulges what he already knows about his cousin, the story of him losing it on a university president, Alexandra hardly knows how to respond and immediately shuts him up. We see that Atticus has indeed shared the family history with his children, but not the sanitized version his sister prefers.

Scout's tears in response to Atticus's uncomfortable speech about the family's standing illustrate the shock a child feels when everything comfortable and normal to them is suddenly uprooted. Atticus manages to reassure her by abandoning his silly discourse, but Scout will soon learn that discomfort is not always alleviated, but it must be confronted.

CHAPTER 14

What happens?

Aunt Alexandra tones down her lessons in family pride to the kids, especially as the sentiment of family shame is directed at them due to their father's defense of Tom Robinson. As the details of the case become more familiar to Scout, she asks Atticus what rape is, and he responds truthfully, though Scout still does not fully understand. In this conversation, Scout also recounts to Atticus their visit to Calpurnia's church and her own desire to visit Cal's home. Alexandra is shocked and does not allow Atticus to respond before uttering a decisive no to Scout's request.

Later, Scout overhears a conversation between Atticus and Alexandra about the latter's desire to get rid of Calpurnia, an idea Atticus adamantly rejects. When Jem pulls Scout aside to advise her on not upsetting Alexandra, she resents his assumption of an authority role over her. The two end up in a fight, which Atticus has to break up, but they drop the matter when Alexandra irritates both of them.

While going to bed, Scout discovers something in her room. She calls Jem in, and he finds Dill hiding under the bed. Famished, Dill reveals he has run away from home. Jem decides Atticus must know of Dill's presence, so he leaves to call him. Atticus feeds Dill and then informs his aunt of his whereabouts. Everyone is at once shocked and relieved to find him, and it is decided that Dill can sleep in the Finch house that evening. In the middle of the night, he leaves Jem's room to crawl into bed with Scout, where he reveals the real motive behind his fleeing home: as it turned out, he felt unwanted by his mother and her new partner. Before dosing off, Dill tells a story about where babies come from, though it does not involve any sex.

Analysis:

Aunt Alexandra is confirming the fears Scout had of her ruining their happy household. By thwarting her desire to visit Calpurnia's home, Alexandra not only embodies the town's prejudices and conventions, but is imposing them on her relatives. Adding to Scout's frustration is Jem's attempt to act as an authority figure. Scout's young mind does not grasp that Jem himself is negotiating, sometimes clumsily, the territory between childhood and adulthood, and she does not see that his advice to her comes from his evolving understanding of social rules. That Jem fights with her makes it difficult for Scout to understand his growing maturity.

Just as Scout's home life seems as alien as ever, she is granted a respite with the arrival of Dill. Now the adult world that had been creeping into her childhood can be held at bay, at least temporarily. The division between Jem and the other children is more pronounced when he tells his father of Dill's presence. The young man now clearly values responsibility over children's pacts of secrecy.

Key takeaways:

Atticus's honesty is evident even in the way he treats his children. He gives Scout a straightforward definition of rape when she asks and does not try to avoid the heavy topic. Lee again depicts Atticus as an excellent father and an exemplary model of the principle of leading by example.

To Aunt Alexandra, however, Atticus's unorthodox ways threaten to undermine the family's status. Indeed, his assertion that Calpurnia is a member of the family unsettles his sister, but it also forces her to recognize that Jem and Scout were indeed raised by a black woman and, despite their minor oddities, they are good children. While Alexandra has come across as narrow-minded and conventional until this point, her better qualities will begin to reveal themselves—a shift that reinforces the novel's theme of essential goodness.

Lee's wit is expressed in Scout's reaction to overhearing another quibble between Atticus and Alexandra. Realizing they are speaking about her, she feels "The starched walls of a pink cotton penitentiary closing in on me." Scout has yet to find Alexandra's version of southern womanhood anything but stifling.

CHAPTER 15

What happens?

Dill is allowed to stay in Maycomb for the summer, and the children resume their usual summer play. Two days before Tom Robinson's trial is to begin, a group of men, including Sheriff Heck Tate, show up at the Finch home. While Atticus is outside speaking with them, Scout and Jem listen intently at the window, hearing the men discuss Tom and Tate's opinion that he should not be kept in the town jail the night before his trial. When Link Deas tells Atticus that he has everything to lose in representing Tom, Atticus replies curtly and cryptically, "Do you really think so?" Sensing that tension is growing among the group, Jem interrupts the exchange, yelling to Atticus that the phone is ringing, to which Atticus matter-of-factly replies by instructing Jem to answer it. The men leave laughing, and Scout then realizes that they are all people she knows from the town.

Later Aunt Alexandra expresses her concerns about the case to Atticus, a conversation which Scout overhears but does not fully comprehend. When she asks Jem for clarification, he gives little but says that he is worried about Atticus. The next day, Sunday, Tom Robinson is transported to the town jail in Maycomb. That evening, Atticus, equipped with a lamp and an extension cord, announces that he is going out and will be back late and, contrary to his usual practice, he takes the car rather than walking. After they have gone to bed, Scout finds Jem awake and getting dressed with the intention of looking for Atticus. Scout and Dill join him. After checking his office, the children find Atticus perched outside the jail reading a book by the lamplight. Four cars then appear and the men in them tell Atticus to get out of the way. He refuses and reminds them that Sheriff Tate is not far off, though one of them informs Atticus that they have already lured the sheriff out of town. When told that the sheriff's absence changes the matter, Atticus replies, "Do you really think so?" Upon hearing this, Scout leaps from the doorway where she had been hiding with Jem and Dill and runs to Atticus. When Atticus sees the children, he demands they return home at once, but Jem defies his father and insists on staying. One of the men pulls Jem away, but Scout kicks him in the groin.

Scout realizes the men are not the ones who had come to the house the evening before, and she recognizes only one, Mr. Cunningham. Unaware of the seriousness of the situation, Scout greets him politely and asks him about his entailment, and mentions that she goes to school with his son. Silence falls over the group, and Scout suddenly feels self-conscious about what she has said. Moved by her kindness and innocence, Mr. Cunningham reassures Scout and then instructs the men to leave.

Once the group leaves, Tom Robinson's voice is heard inquiring of Atticus whether everything is safe. At this point, Atticus and the children learn that Mr. Underwood, the editor of *The Maycomb Tribune*, had been protecting them with his rifle from his office above the jail. Atticus and the children return home.

Analysis:

The suspense is building in the run-up to the trial. Anxious townspeople turn to Atticus for advice and guidance, and even he exhibits unease and heads to the jail to protect Tom Robinson. That Jem is indeed entering the adult sphere is evident by his own apprehension over his father's safety. His decision to check on Atticus in the middle of the night, and subsequently to defy his father's command to leave, marks his transition from boy to man. Jem is not disrespectful of his father, but wary of the consequences Atticus's precarious situation could have.

Until this chapter, the threat posed to Atticus for his role in defending Tom has been abstract. Now, however, the prospect of real violence is closer than ever before as he stares down an angry mob. Considering the high drama, it is surprising that a young girl's innocence defuses the tension. Applying the social graces learned from her father, to greet people you know and talk about subjects that interest them, Scout kindly addresses Mr. Cunningham and inquires after his entailment. This artless injection of civility shifts the men's attention away from Tom and toward a child who is oblivious to the peril at hand. If these angry men are unable to see a black man as a human being, they cannot fail to perceive humanity in a well-meaning schoolgirl who is out late only to check on her beloved father. The novel's message is clear: civility can curb evil intentions and expose human goodness.

Key takeaways:

An entailed estate is one whose inheritance has been limited to a specified succession of heirs. The heir of an entailed estate cannot sell it or alter the line of its successors. It is unclear how Atticus helped Mr. Cunningham with his entailment, but it is normal for attorneys to handle matters related to such a restriction.

Throughout the novel, Atticus comes across as profoundly aware of the motives behind his actions and behaviors. His use of the Socratic-like question, "Do you really think so?" therefore seems strange. On the two occasions he uses this phrase, he is responding to someone questioning the situation he has gotten himself into. But rather than burdening himself with answering a futile question, he turns the query back on the questioner in a philosophic tone. His rhetorical question no doubt expresses Atticus's conviction that he is right.

CHAPTER 16

What happens?

The night's events are reviewed at breakfast the next morning. Atticus expresses surprise at Mr. Underwood's support, claiming that everyone knows "He despises Negroes." Aunt Alexandra reproaches Atticus for speaking that way in front of Calpurnia, to which Atticus quickly replies that Cal already knows this and that she is privy to all of their mealtime discussions. But Alexandra is worried their conversation might become the topic of gossip among the black community, to which Atticus wryly retorts that perhaps whites shouldn't partake in so much gossip-worthy behavior.

Scout inquires about Mr. Cunningham and why he wanted to hurt Atticus. Atticus explains to Scout that her appearance the night before had made Mr. Cunningham consider the situation from Atticus's perspective and his empathy led him away from the confrontation. Soon Dill arrives, reporting that the whole town is astir with news of the children fighting off the mob. The children head out to the porch where they see nearly the entire town and county heading to the courthouse. They soon learn that Miss Maudie refuses to observe the trial, though Miss Stephanie Crawford can't manage to keep herself from it.

After lunch, in defiance of their father's order, Jem, Scout and Dill head to the courthouse. When they arrive, the crowds are waiting outside, and the children begin observing some of the town's more eccentric inhabitants—above all, Mr. Dolphus Raymond. Drinking whiskey from a brown paper bag and sitting with the black community, Mr. Raymond piques the kids' interest. Jem explains that he comes from an old, established family and was once engaged, but his fiancé killed herself, so they say, when she learned of his black mistress and illegitimate children. Since then, he feels more comfortable among the black community and is almost always drunk. Responding to Scout's question of what a "mixed" child is, Jem explains that it means they are both black and white and sad because they are not accepted by either community. This confuses Scout, who wonders aloud how anyone can know whether they are fully white.

In the courtroom, Scout learns for the first time that Atticus was appointed by the judge to defend Tom Robinson and wonders why he had never mentioned this point before. Since there is no space for them in the courtroom, the children head upstairs with Reverend Sykes to the balcony where blacks can observe. Here they listen to the testimony of Sheriff Heck Tate.

Analysis:

The parade of white people heading to the courthouse highlights the vulgarity of their desire to attend the trial. They are going to gawk at an innocent man whose only crime is being black in the American South. It is important that Miss Maudie refuses to attend and that the children sit in the "colored" balcony to observe the trial. None of them are part of Maycomb's racist whites who have already condemned Tom Robinson and attend the trial only to have such condemnation confirmed.

Jem's role as Scout and Dill's interpreter of the adult world is fixed in this chapter. He gives the children a background profile of the enigmatic Mr. Dolphus Raymond and explains to them what a "mixed" child is. However, it is Scout's inquisitiveness, which is still unpolluted by society's expectations, that produces the most thoughtful remark in the children's discussion: how is anyone sure of being a hundred percent white? While Jem and Scout now represent different life stages, emerging adult maturity and childhood innocence respectively, it is the latter whose naïveté results in the most probing logic.

Key takeaways:

While Alexandra is eventually redeemed to a certain extent, she will likely never close the gap between herself and black people. Her fear that the family's breakfast conversation could end up in the rumor mills of the black community shows how different her thinking is from the rest of the family, who act naturally and speak freely in front of Calpurnia. Unlike Alexandra, their public personas are no different from their private personas.

Atticus's comment that everyone knows Mr. Underwood "Despises Negroes," which he states in front of Cal, is refreshing in its spontaneity and artlessness. It is evident that Atticus considers Cal an equal and knows that she will understand his remark for exactly what it is: a statement of truth.

The balcony reserved for "colored" people was not merely a custom of small-town Alabama. In 1930s America, racial segregation was backed up by law and institutionalized. Blacks and whites had different schools, churches, transportation means, medical care and even entrances to buildings. Segregation was not eradicated until the Civil Rights era.

CHAPTER 17

What happens?

Questioned by the prosecutor, Mr. Gilmer, Sheriff Tate gives an account of the events that took place on November 21st of the previous year. He was fetched by Bob Ewell and brought to the Ewell house where he found Mayella, the eldest child, badly beaten. The Ewells claimed that Tom Robinson beat and raped her, and Mr. Tate promptly arrested the suspect. Under cross-examination by Atticus, Mr. Tate admits that no one called a doctor and, at Atticus's prompting, he establishes that Mayella's right eye was blackened, the right side of her face was bruised, and that there were hand marks around her entire neck.

Bob Ewell is the next witness called to the stand. Upon seeing Mr. Ewell, Scout reflects on the Ewell family and their living conditions, which she once saw when she and Atticus disposed of their Christmas tree at the town dump. She realizes that Mr. Ewell has nothing and is no better than his black neighbors, except that his skin happened to be white.

Mr. Ewell, who is rude and cocky on the stand, claims he came running home when he heard Mayella screaming and, from the window, saw Tom Robinson raping her. Once the judge resumes order to the shocked crowd, Mr. Ewell explains that he rushed into the house after Tom, but failed to catch him and then ran to Sheriff Tate instead. When the prosecutor completes his questioning, Mr. Ewell gets up to return to his seat and bumps into Atticus who had risen to begin his questioning. After Mr. Ewell returned to the stand, Atticus inquires whether anyone called a doctor, to which the witness responds that there was no reason to do so. Atticus then has Mr. Ewell confirm Sheriff Tate's account of Mayella's injuries and asks him whether he can read or write. Mr. Ewell proves his literacy to the court by writing his name, after which Atticus points out that he is left-handed. Though Scout is confused about Atticus's strategy, Jem is growing ever more confident of his father's victory.

Analysis:

At last the trial begins, and Lee covers its intricate details over several successive chapters. It is a testament to Lee's excellent writing ability that she manages to build up suspense for an event the outcome of which is already known to all including the reader. She understands that the verdict is not what everyone has been waiting to hear; what is paramount is learning the details and meeting the figures involved—the concrete information that has remained elusive throughout the novel.

Without much attention to anything else, Lee lets the trial unfold. For the first time, Bob Ewell comes to life in the story, and he lives up to his reputation as an ignorant, arrogant and "trashy," to use Atticus's term for him, individual. Mr. Ewell is in on the game in that he knows an all-white jury will never believe a black man over a white man, and his arrogance betrays his feeling that they are all just going through the motions to reach the inevitable outcome.

Even though Mr. Ewell is correct in predicting the trial's outcome, he still becomes a victim of Atticus's wit and intelligence by being tricked into revealing his left-handedness. Though officialdom will declare Tom Robinson guilty, Atticus's maneuvers reveal the true culprit, and Mr. Ewell will eventually be punished in the court of public opinion.

Key takeaways:

Surprisingly, the most disturbing element of this chapter is not necessarily Mr. Ewell's behavior on the stand, but Sheriff Tate's testimony. The good-hearted law officer conveys two unsettling points: first, that he did not call a doctor; second, that he arrested Tom Robinson after hearing

Mr. Ewell's account of the alleged attack. Though a well-meaning individual, the sheriff let Maycomb's prevailing prejudices guide his thinking on that evening. Rather than seeking to verify the Ewells' account, either by calling a doctor or seeking other proof, Tate merely takes the word of a white man over a black man. Apparently, he too sometimes suffers from "Maycomb's usual disease."

Mr. Ewell's real name, Robert E. Lee Ewell, is farcical, for the real Robert E. Lee, the Confederate general who fought for the South despite personally opposing slavery, was an honorable and much esteemed figure, an undisputed hero. Bob Ewell is quite the opposite—racist, hateful and immoral.

CHAPTER 18

What happens?

Mayella now takes the stand and submits to questions from the prosecutor, Mr. Gilmer. She at first remains quiet, uttering only curt answers, but soon bursts into tears when the judge encourages her to tell her story. She admits that she is scared of Atticus, but the judge insists that scaring her is not Atticus's intention and that he will prevent him from doing so if he tries. When she finally testifies, she claims she was on the porch when Tom Robinson was walking home and asked him to break up a piece of furniture for kindling. She went into the house to get him a nickel, but he followed her, attacking and raping her.

It is then Atticus's turn to question Mayella. She is offended by his politeness, mistaking it for ridicule. Atticus asks about her family, her schooling and whether she has friends. Mayella again thinks Atticus is making fun of her because she does not understand why she should have any friends. Atticus also wonders whether her father has ever beaten her, which she denies. When questioned about Tom's alleged attack, Mayella confuses some of the facts, but identifies Tom as the suspect when asked by Atticus to do so. When Tom rises to be seen clearly by his accuser, it becomes clear to everyone that Tom's left arm is shriveled and useless. Reverend Sykes explains to the children that Tom got his arm caught in a cotton gin when he was a child. Atticus asks Mayella how Tom could have attacked her and invites her to reconsider her previous testimony, but she refuses. Atticus then increases the intensity of his questioning, asking Mayella if she screamed not at Tom, but only once she saw her father in the window, and whether it was actually her father who beat her. After listening to these questions in silence, Mayella finally erupts, restating her accusations against Tom and accusing the men of being cowards if they do not convict him. After her testimony, the court recesses.

Analysis:

If Mr. Ewell offends everyone, including the reader, Mayella Ewell elicits pity. While she recounts her manufactured version of events concerning the night of the alleged attack, Atticus's astute questioning reveals this young woman's actual tragic story: she is the eldest daughter of a poor, ignorant drunk who beats her and, as punishment for finding her alone with a black man, forces her to lie in order to convict an innocent man. Though Mayella cannot see it, she has more in common with Tom Robinson, a fellow victim, than with her abusive father, as both of them suffer at the hands of that despicable man who is basking in the temporary recognition he has gained due to the trial.

This chapter helps the reader understand Atticus's unforgiving and harsh opinion of Mr. Ewell, which he expresses throughout the novel and which always seems out of character for him. But Mayella's testimony reveals the depth of her father's wickedness, for she is so isolated from and de-sensitized to humanity that she believes Atticus rude for calling her "Miss Mayella" or "Ma'am," and fails to make sense of his question about having friends. Depressingly, Atticus's belief that civility brings out one's inner goodness proves incorrect in this case. Mayella is vicious toward him and renews her brutal accusation against Tom Robinson.

Even though Mayella sticks to her story and thus secures a guilty verdict, she is burying herself in front of Maycomb society, just as her father did with his testimony. Revealing her ignorance, harshness and coarse nature, she seals her role as a social outcast worthy of little more than complete ostracism.

Key takeaways:

Scout's insights about Mayella's sad existence make her seem far beyond her years. Perhaps because she has an excellent father, Scout pities Mayella for the father she ended up with, who has made her into "The loneliest person in the world." While Atticus is always helping Scout learn how to live in society, Mr. Ewell draws his children farther away from it.

Jem's response to discovering Tom Robinson's disability is at once heartening and disheartening. It pleases him for his father's sake, but also misleadingly convinces him that Atticus will prevail. Though Jem understands the case's details and the lawyers' strategies much better than Scout and Dill do, his residual childhood innocence prevents him from seeing that the outcome is inevitable. Atticus proves to everyone that Tom Robinson is innocent, but what Jem cannot see is that proof is no obstacle to racism.

CHAPTER 19

What happens?

When the lawyers and judge return to the courtroom, Atticus calls Tom Robinson to the witness stand. His injured left arm becomes more evident as he cannot manage to place it on the Bible to take the oath. After some simple background questions, Atticus hones in on the night of the alleged attack. Tom explains that Mayella had not asked him to chop up a piece of furniture; he had done that for her several months earlier, and he explains that Mayella often asked him to come inside the fence to do small jobs for her, though he always declined payment.

Describing the night in question, Tom claims he was returning home when Mayella asked him to come in to fix a door, but the door was fine when he saw it. Tom then realized that none of the other children were home, and Mayella explained to him that she sent them out for ice cream after having saved for the treat a full year. She then asked him to get something down from the wardrobe, but when he stepped on a chair to grab it, Mayella put her arms around his leg causing him to jump and knock the chair over. Mayella then tried to hug and kiss him, claiming she had never kissed a man before and saying that what her father did to her did not count. Tom was asking Mayella to move aside when her father appeared at the window yelling, "You goddamn whore, I'll kill ya." Tom ran away after that.

As Mr. Gilmer approaches to question Tom, Mr. Link Deas rises from the crowd and claims that Tom had always been a good worker who never caused any trouble. Mr. Gilmer gets Tom to admit that, despite his left hand, he is physically strong. As Mr. Gilmer presses Tom on why he did so many favors for Mayella, Tom admits he felt sorry for her. Surprised by this response, Mr. Gilmer makes sure the jury has enough time to register it and to show their disgust at a black man feeling sorry for a white woman. Mr. Gilmer then tries to prove Tom's guilt by the fact that he ran away from the scene.

At this point, Dill is crying uncontrollably and Scout escorts him outside where he explains that Mr. Gilmer's treatment of Tom sickened him. Mr. Dolphus Raymond listens to their conversation and intervenes to agree with Dill.

Analysis:

The novel's theme that appearances are deceiving is illustrated profoundly in this chapter. The accused rapist, who has been silent until now, reveals himself as an honest, hard-working, sincere and moral human being—qualities that have nothing to do with the color of his skin. He bravely recounts the truth about what happened that fateful night and tells all that Mayella had made sexual advances toward him. In questioning Tom, Atticus pieces together the whole story: Tom entered the house to help Mayella; she kissed him, her abusive (both physically and sexually, as we now learn) father beat her for attempting to seduce a black man, and now the family sought to rid itself of guilt by finding a scapegoat.

Despite his precarious position, Tom shows compassion for Mayella, but allows his emotions to run over when he lets slip that he felt sorry her. If there were any hope that Atticus might convince the jury to do the right thing (which there never was), it was all gone now. Tom's empathy for Mayella sealed his fate, for Maycomb's white society cannot tolerate a black man pitying a white woman. They have no choice but to retreat back into their rigid social/racial order, even if that means taking the word of a scoundrel over a decent man.

While Atticus's questioning of Tom may have led many people to consider factors besides the color of his skin, Mr. Gilmer's cross-examination ensures that everyone will remember the defendant is black. He calls him "Boy" and ascribes to him the stereotypical vices racists attribute to all black men: lying, violent behavior and a desire for white women. This ugly sequence proves too harsh for Dill's childlike constitution, and he reacts to this frightening episode as most children react to fear: with tears.

Key takeaways:

This chapter highlights again the power tradition has over reason. Though there is no way Tom could have hit Mayella with this left hand or strangled her neck with both hands, these facts do not exculpate him. Indeed, Tom cannot be exonerated because he is not guilty of a crime, as everyone knows—he is guilty of having the wrong skin color.

The only reasonable evidence the prosecution has against Tom is that he ran from the scene of the alleged crime. Running away is usually a sign of guilt. But the grim reality of the American South of the 1930s is that a black man would have had little chance of being believed had he stayed. Tom was not running from a crime; he was running for his life.

CHAPTER 20

What happens?

To help calm Dill, Mr. Raymond offers him a sip of the drink in his paper bag, which Dill discovers is merely Coca-Cola. Mr. Raymond explains to Dill and Scout that he pretends to be drunk in order to give the townspeople a ready explanation for his unusual behavior. Scout questions Mr. Raymond's dishonesty, but he points out that the people of Maycomb would never understand that he lives with the black community because he prefers to; they only comprehend drunkenness as an excuse for his choices. Mr. Raymond confides his secret in Dill and Scout because of their innocence, for they have not yet been polluted by the world's realities.

When the children return to the courtroom, Atticus is wrapping up his closing remarks. Uncharacteristically, Atticus loosens his tie, removes his jacket and unbuttons his vest and begins speaking in more familiar tones rather than in legal jargon. He claims the case never should have gone to trial as there is no evidence a rape actually took place, Mayella is motivated by guilt over her desire for Tom, and she was clearly beaten by someone who hits with his left hand. Atticus then reveals that the prosecution is relying on the jury's prejudices to believe a white man over a black man, but he appeals to their intelligence not to fall for that type of thinking. Quoting Thomas Jefferson that all men are created equal, Atticus implores the jury to do their duty "In the name of God." After Atticus sits down, Calpurnia suddenly appears in the courtroom.

Analysis:

The narrator spares the reader the experience of hearing all of Mr. Gilmer's cross-examination and gives her young protagonist a break from the adult nature of the trial. Scout's recess from adult reality is not long, however, as Mr. Raymond reveals his secret to the children. In some ways, Mr. Raymond and the Finch family are alike: they both detest the town's racist attitudes and believe in the dignity of all races. But Mr. Raymond's method of dealing with the town stands in stark contrast to the Finch family's, especially Atticus's, ways. He permits Maycomb to use drunkenness as an excuse for this behavior and thus avoids confrontation and maintains peace, though his means are cynical. Atticus, on the other hand, hides behind nothing. Though his views go against the town's grain, he stands by them uncompromisingly. At the same time, Atticus maintains a relative peace with his fellow townspeople by emphasizing the essential goodness in everyone. Though he is inflexible in his beliefs, his principled ways and fair judgment of others command the town's respect.

Atticus's closing argument epitomizes his definition of courage: giving your best even when defeat is certain. But defeat or victory no longer seem defined by the verdict alone. Atticus's final remarks to the jury go beyond the limit of this particular trial and address a broader audience—the entire town. Here he puts Maycomb on trial, and after establishing again Tom's innocence, he appeals to the town's best qualities, encouraging them to discover the honor and confidence in themselves to do the right thing. Remarkably, Atticus's closing argument is in no way cynical, but optimistic in its belief that everyone in that room, but above all the jury, had it in himself or herself to do what is right. Here again Lee returns to innate goodness and, despite the grim circumstances, does not leave the reader or her young protagonist in despair.

Key takeaways:

The difference between the town's treatment of Mr. Raymond and Tom Robinson is unsettling. Both crossed racial boundaries—Tom by entering the Ewell house and by feeling sorry for Mayella; Mr. Raymond by living among the blacks—but only one of them, the black man, suffers for his alleged transgression. The lesson is harsh: white men of means and heritage are held to a different standard than black men with nothing. The town excuses Mr. Raymond, and he provides them with the tools to do so, but condemns Tom.

Judge Taylor's role in the trial is enigmatic. He maintains order and guides the witnesses, but remains passive about the blatant miscarriage of justice unfolding before his eyes. When Link Deas blurts out his good opinion of Tom Robinson, Judge Taylor punishes him with expulsion from the courthouse. The prosecuting attorney and the plaintiffs, however, are permitted to convince a jury to convict a man because he is black.

Calpurnia's appearance immediately following Atticus's closing remarks is important symbolically. Her march down the room's center aisle divides the white audience—a sign of Atticus's attempt to undo the ingrained herd mentality that governs this group's thinking about race.

CHAPTER 21

What happens?

Calpurnia came to the courthouse to inform Atticus that the children are missing. Mr. Underwood tells him his kids are in the balcony, where all eyes now turn. The children return home with Calpurnia, but Atticus grants them permission to come back after dinner.

Back at the courthouse, the children take their seats in the balcony and, along with everyone else, await the jury's decision. Jem expresses his confidence in impending victory to Reverend Sykes, who conveys a far more skeptical attitude. Over the three-hour wait, Scout falls asleep and wakes up to the memory of Atticus shooting the mad dog. The jury returns and issues a verdict of guilty. Atticus speaks briefly with Tom and then collects his belongings to exit the courthouse. As he is leaving, everyone in the "colored balcony" rises as a sign of respect for Atticus.

Analysis:

With the re-injection of Calpurnia into the narrative at this crucial moment, Lee draws attention to the stark contrast between Maycomb's conventional wisdom and the Finch family logic. While the town is on the brink of reinforcing its rigid racial hierarchy by punishing a man for nothing other than being black, Calpurnia, the black housekeeper, is scolding Jem for attending the trial on their walk home. This is perhaps the clearest depiction of how unorthodox a family the Finches were.

Scout's memory/dream right before the issuing of the verdict is telling. It symbolizes Atticus's ability to see beyond the town's prejudices and conventions to what is right and just. He is unable to guide his fellow townspeople in the same direction, however, because his gun is without bullets.

In other words, he cannot kill the mad dog: "Maycomb's usual sickness."

Key takeaways:

Aunt Alexandra still seems to be part of Maycomb's static fabric in this chapter as the horror she expresses when she discovers the children had been at the trial derives more from her fear of what people might think of the family than from her concern that the content was inappropriate for the children.

The optimism that Jem conveys to Reverend Sykes is painful to read as it is evident that Lee is setting him up for a fall. He is still too idealistic to pick up the clues in the more experienced Reverend's skepticism.

It is telling that Jem and Scout have to be told to stand up while their father exits the courtroom. It shows they still see him in familiar family terms and are not yet fully aware of the important role he plays in Maycomb.

CHAPTER 22

What happens?

Jem is unable to control his anger over the injustice of the verdict and cries during the walk home with his father. Aunt Alexandra expresses her disappointment at the verdict to soothe her brother, but manages to reproach him for allowing his children to observe the trial. Atticus defends his decision, exclaiming that racism is as much a part of the town's fabric as are missionary teas.

After a night's rest, Atticus regains hope and seems more confident that Tom will win the appeal. Calpurnia prepared a large breakfast as she found numerous gifts of food on the steps left their by grateful members of Maycomb's black community. With tears welling up in his eyes, Atticus asks Calpurnia to thank everyone for their thoughtful gestures. Atticus leaves and Dill takes his place at the table, devouring his untouched breakfast.

Outside, the children see Miss Stephanie Crawford recounting the trial to Miss Maudie and Mr. Avery. Seeing Jem's disappointment, Miss Maudie invites the children in for cake, where they discover that she has made a large cake especially for Jem. Discussing the trial, Jem expresses his disillusionment with Maycomb and how it no longer seems the town is full of good people. But Miss Maudie points out that many individuals gave their support to Tom Robinson, including Judge Taylor, who purposely chose Atticus to represent Tom in order to give him the best defense possible. Miss Maudie also explains that their father succeeded in making the jury think, as no other lawyer could have gotten a jury of white men to take three hours to reach a verdict. In her eyes, this latter fact represents a modest victory, or at least a step forward.

After leaving Miss Maudie's house, Aunt Alexandra calls the children in off the street out of fear of Mr. Ewell, who that morning, they learn, spat in Atticus's face.

Analysis:

This chapter begins the family's road to recovery after the emotional trial. Though Jem is more mature than Dill, he cannot help but also respond with tears to the crushing defeat. He had allowed his hopes to grow too high and now the raw emotion triggered by the unexpected outcome brought forth a rain of tears. Atticus wisely lets his son cry it out.

The morning restores a degree of hope, and the gifts left on the family's back porch are more evidence of people's goodness, despite the unsettling verdict. While Miss Stephanie Crawford prattles on about the trial even as the children approach, Miss Maudie knows not to raise the delicate topic, but to soothe her young friends with something sweet and comforting.

For Jem, the verdict is reason to despair and give over to disillusionment, but the more experienced Miss Maudie provides him with some perspective. Though the jury found Tom guilty, change was still taking place, though in a slow or furtive manner. That the jurors spent three hours to make up their minds is a sort of victory and a sign that Maycomb is reflecting more on itself and its ways.

Another small victory is Mr. Ewell's apparent despair. Though the jury convicted Tom, the town has evidently rejected the Ewells, and Bob Ewell feels threatened.

Key takeaways:

The image of Miss Stephanie gossiping is sad in that it represents the immediate resumption of routine after the interruption to it caused by the trial. Miss Stephanie symbolizes the town's static elements.

Her fixed position contrasts sharply with Jem's emotional growth. Though dejected, he seeks answers from Miss Maudie and is open to listening to her reasoning. Jem himself comes to represent hope.

CHAPTER 23

What happens?

Atticus refuses to consider Mr. Ewell's actions in a serious way until he realizes that his children are actually quite scared for him. He manages to reassure them and to dispel their fears. Tom Robinson is now in the Enfield Prison awaiting the appeal process. Responding to Scout's query about Tom's fate if he were to lose on appeal, Atticus explains that he will be put to death. Jem objects to the death penalty for rape, while Atticus, though he does not disagree with his son, is more upset over a jury convicting a man for a crime punishable by death based only on circumstantial evidence and over the message the jury's decision reinforces: whites always prevail over blacks. Jem wonders why more open-minded people, such as Miss Maudie, never end up on juries, but Atticus reminds him that women cannot be jurors and that many men don't want to find themselves in the position of making a decision that might upset the town. Despite these unsettling realities, Atticus is hopeful in knowing that it was one of Mr. Cunningham's relatives who kept the jury from issuing an instant conviction, even though the night before this same man had showed up at the town jail with the intention of lynching Tom.

Upon hearing this, Scout determines to befriend Walter Cunningham, a plan her class-conscious Aunt Alexandra roundly dismisses, warning Scout that the Cunninghams are not of the same social caliber as the Finches. Jem drags off the infuriated Scout in order to avoid a confrontation and then explains to his sister what he finally understands about Maycomb's social ranks: there are people like them, country people like the Cunninghams, trash like the Ewells, and, finally, the blacks. Each group wants to distance itself from the one below it. Reflecting on this ugly reality, Jem claims he understands why Boo Radley chooses to remain locked inside his house.

Analysis:

The exchange between Atticus and Jem over legal issues shows how Jem is maturing into a man like his father, though he still has a long road ahead of him. While Atticus is thoughtful and reflective about his opinions, seeing the issues from many sides, Jem is absolute, driven more by his still-raw emotions than by his reason.

Jem's evolution from his younger self at the beginning of the novel is evident in his remarks about placing Miss Maudie on a jury. His ideas about gender roles are expanding, and it is heartening that he thinks of Miss Maudie not as a woman, but as an open-minded person. Her thinking contrasts sharply with Aunt Alexandra's, who forbids Scout from befriending Walter Cunningham solely on the grounds that his family is beneath theirs. That Atticus does not intervene in this conversation confirms his confidence that his children will not be persuaded by such ill-judged logic.

Jem has also changed his thinking concerning Alexandra. Rather than encouraging Scout not to upset their aunt, as he did previously, he merely advises his sister to avoid her. Jem's lesson to Scout about Maycomb's social order is anyway more useful than their aunt's interpretation, for Jem understands how irrational it is, as it depends on always despising the group below.

Key takeaways:

For once, Atticus's advice to stand in someone else's shoes—in this instance Bob Ewell's—fails, for he is unable to comprehend the depth of Mr. Ewell's wickedness. Only Aunt Alexandra, whose views on Maycomb society usually seem so foreign to the Finches, understands that Mr. Ewell's threats are not empty. Her role as the family protector is finally useful.

Atticus's advice to Jem and Scout, "Don't fool yourselves—it's all adding up and one of these days we're going to pay the bill for it," is no doubt Lee's way of referencing the Civil Rights Movement, which was in full swing when she published the novel in 1960.

The chapter's end, when Jem comments on the logic behind Boo Radley's reclusiveness, marks a shift back to the first plot dealing with the children's fascination and exchanges with him. In these final chapters, we shall see the two stories become intertwined.

CHAPTER 24

What happens?

Aunt Alexandra hosts a missionary tea at the Finch home and permits Calpurnia to serve the group. Since the boys are off skinny-dipping, Scout is at home and offers to help Cal, who lets her carry the coffee into the living room. Scout remains to join the group, though she resolves to stay silent until someone speaks to her. Miss Stephanie Crawford begins questioning her in a teasing manner, but she manages to maintain her composure with the aid of Miss Maudie.

Mrs. Grace Merriweather discusses the Mruna tribe and the efforts of a valiant missionary to Christianize it. Without noticing any contradiction in her thinking, she continues on about how she must reprimand her black servants when they are cranky. Another guest picks up this thread by remarking on the innate immorality of blacks, and Mrs. Merriweather rejoins with the comment that some people of Maycomb think they are helping matters when all they are actually doing is making things worse. Realizing they are speaking of Atticus, Miss Maudie confronts the ladies, asking wryly whether this person's food "sticks" while going down—an explicit reference to Atticus as they are eating in his home. Aunt Alexandra is grateful to Miss Maudie.

Atticus returns home early and asks Alexandra to come to the kitchen. He announces to her, Calpurnia, Miss Maudie and Scout that Tom Robinson was killed while trying to escape from prison. Atticus and Calpurnia leave to inform Tom's wife, while Alexandra expresses her disappointment in the townspeople who place the burden of doing the right thing on Atticus alone.

Analysis:

The post-trial emotions still seem raw in this genteel gathering of Maycomb ladies. Mrs. Merriweather and others uphold the town's hypocrisy, expressing sorrow over the plight of the poor Mruna tribe, while lamenting having to deal with their grouchy black servants, or, as she insensitively puts it, "A sulky darky." Mrs. Merriweather uses this opportunity to indirectly scold Atticus for attempting to upset the racial hierarchy.

These comments test Aunt Alexandra's patience and gentility. Though she remains composed in front of the Maycomb ladies, she issues a bitter invective against the town in the privacy of the kitchen after learning of Tom's death. No longer wavering, Alexandra has firmly staked her ground on the side of her family, not the town, and she returns to face her refined company with the support of Miss Maudie and Scout, who comes to see her aunt in a new light.

Key takeaways:

The Mruna tribe is fictional but based on the African tribes visited by many Christian missionaries in the early twentieth century.

The freshness of Scout's mind is clear in her response to Mrs. Merriweather's statement about forgiving those who have done wrong to others. Scout thinks she is speaking of Mayella, who wrongfully accused Tom Robinson; however, Mrs. Merriweather, whose mind is polluted with "Maycomb's usual disease," had been referring to Helen Robinson, who committed the immoral act of being black.

It is clear that Scout is beginning to negotiate her way in the world of southern femininity, especially as she finds supportive allies in the group—first Miss Maudie and then, unexpectedly, Aunt Alexandra. Her transition to the female world is still incomplete, however, as she continues to don her britches underneath her lovely pink dress.

Mrs. Merriweather makes a reference to "That Mrs. Roosevelt," meaning Mrs. Eleanor Roosevelt, an American social activist and wife of President Franklin Delano Roosevelt. In 1939, at the Southern Conference for Human Welfare in Birmingham, Alabama, Mrs. Roosevelt defied segregation laws by sitting in the aisle between the black and white sections.

CHAPTER 25

What happens?

Though it is September, Jem and Scout are still sleeping on the back porch. Jem stops Scout from killing a small bug, and she is convinced he is becoming more like a girl. Scout then recalls a conversation she had with Dill before his departure. The day Atticus told them of Tom's death, the boys came upon him while they were returning from swimming. They hopped in the car with him and Calpurnia and went to the Robinson's home. Mrs. Robinson fainted when she learned of Tom's death, and Atticus and Calpurnia had to carry her into the house. While the boys returned home with Atticus, they heard voices yelling at them from the Ewell house.

The news of Tom's death remains the main subject of town gossip for several days, and the topic is fuelled by a biting editorial written by Mr. Underwood in *The Maycomb Tribune*. The paper's owner and editor claims that Tom's conviction was due to racism and that there was never any hope for a fair trial.

The Finch family soon learns Bob Ewell's response to the news of Tom's death: one down, two to go.

Analysis:

This chapter sketches out several important developments and builds suspense toward the novel's dramatic end. Jem now fully embraces his young adulthood, and his conscientiousness is evident when he stops Scout from killing the roly-poly bug. Still sensitive to Tom Robinson's fate, Jem can't bear to witness another injustice inflicted upon an innocent, defenseless creature. Absorbed in her puerile logic, Scout can make sense of Jem's actions only in black-and-white terms: being upset by the smashing of a bug is girly.

Mr. Underwood's scathing editorial establishes that Maycomb's previously inert socio-racial codes are now experiencing some movement, though whether his column will have any real effect besides marking dissension in the white community is unknown.

Recording the yells directed at Atticus from the Ewell house and Bob Ewell's ominous reaction to Tom's death, Lee strongly suggests that a clash between the Finch and Ewells clans is imminent.

Key takeaways:

In his column, Mr. Underwood likens Tom's death to, "The senseless slaughter of songbirds," another reference to the novel's title and to the theme of inflicting injustice on innocents. Mr. Underwood's transformation from one who "Despises Negroes" to one who challenges the town's racism conveys a message of hope: the oppression of Maycomb's ingrained prejudices can be escaped.

In this chapter, the narrator makes an offhand reference to the section of "Colored News" in *The Maycomb Tribune*. Here we see that segregation surfaced even in the newspapers as information was divided by its relevance to the different races.

CHAPTER 26

What happens?

When school resumes, Scout and Jem turn their attention again to the Radley house, which they pass each day. Scout's feelings toward Boo have matured and she regrets their previous curiosity about him and misses his gifts. She tells Atticus that she would like eventually to see her reclusive neighbor. Annoyed, Atticus reminds Scout that they almost got shot in their efforts to see Boo, thus revealing that he knew all along it was them creeping around the Radley yard the evening Nathan Radley fired his shotgun.

While discussing current events in class one day, Scout's teacher, Miss Gates, talks to the children about Adolf Hitler and the persecution of the Jews. Scout recalls Atticus's dislike of Hitler, and later that evening asks whether it is all right to hate him, to which Atticus responds that it is not right to hate anyone. Unable to communicate adequately her thoughts to Atticus, Scout seeks out Jem. She tells him that Miss Gates thinks it is wrong for Hitler to persecute the Jews, but she cannot reconcile her teacher's concern for the Jews with her disdain for the blacks in Maycomb. She remembers that while leaving the courthouse after Tom's trial, she overheard Miss Gates saying, "It's time somebody taught them a lesson." Growing emotional, Jem's only response is that Scout should never again speak to him about the trial. The dejected Scout seeks comfort with Atticus, who explains to her that Jem still cannot comprehend the injustices that took place in that trial.

Analysis:

In sharing Scout's much-altered views of Boo Radley, Lee is setting up their eventual encounter at the novel's end. That the young protagonist is no longer scared of her neighbor is a sign that Tom Robinson's trial has shifted her perspective on life and clarified what is actually scary in the world. Rather than a source of fear, Boo is now a curiosity for her, someone she had almost met on one occasion and whom she now longs to know.

Scout's confusion about Miss Gates highlights Jem's post-trial transformation. The guilty verdict cut the ground out from under Jem by undermining everything he held as true. Now any mere mention of the trial evokes a bitter recollection of its grave consequences. Though Jem is maturing, he has not yet come to understand life's complexities, especially how good can still exist in the evil people of Maycomb who condemned Tom to die.

Key takeaways:

Scout mentions that "Atticus didn't see how anything could happen." For the first time, Atticus's sophisticated understanding of human nature fails him. Perhaps his belief that some good exists in everyone blinds him to the real threat posed by Mr. Ewell. Or, by making her most insightful character oblivious of any impending danger, Lee is further building the suspense to the story's denouement.

The irony of Miss Gates' discussion of democracy following questions about Hitler is palpable. She praises Scout for defining the idea so well: "Equal rights for all, special privileges for none." She fails, however, to see Maycomb's own hypocrisy concerning equal rights. Even when Cecil Jacobs asserts that there is no reason to persecute Jews because, "They're white, ain't they," Miss Gates neglects the real lesson she should impart to her students.

CHAPTER 27

What happens?

Most of Maycomb has put Tom's trial behind them, but Mr. Ewell continues to stew over it. After losing his job with the WPA, he resumes his threats toward Atticus and anyone associated with the trial. On a Sunday evening, he breaks into Judge Taylor's home. He also taunts Helen Robinson on her way to the job Mr. Link Deas gives her. Upon learning of this, Mr. Deas accompanies Helen home one evening and threatens the Ewell family. Mr. Ewell follows Helen to work again, but backs off once Mr. Deas yells at him.

Atticus continues believing Mr. Ewell is all bark and no bite, and the family follows its normal routine. Scout is preparing for Halloween as Mrs. Merriweather has planned a pageant at the school and Scout has agreed to play a ham in a production celebrating Maycomb's agricultural products. Scout parades around in her costume at home for Atticus and Aunt Alexandra and then heads off to the school accompanied by Jem.

Analysis:

While the return to routine likely comforts the Finches, it also signals a return to the normal Maycomb ways, which, to the knowing Atticus, should be a sign of the real danger his family is in. If everything is the same again, then Mr. Ewell is still his wicked self. Menacing warnings are all about Atticus: the incident at Judge Taylor's house and the harassing of Helen Robinson. But the family patriarch remains steadfast in his conviction that Mr. Ewell poses no threat. Scout's account of the misdeeds committed at last year's Halloween and the town's intention to avoid a repeat of the same problem this year provides a model of the anticipatory, preventative thinking Atticus should be applying to his family's current situation.

Key takeaways:

The National Recovery Act (actually the National Industrial Recovery Act) was put into effect in 1933 under President Roosevelt in an effort to help the nation recover from the Great Depression. It approved a 3.3 billion-dollar budget to be used for public works.

The WPA (Work Projects Administration) was one of President Roosevelt's New Deal agencies, which employed millions of out-of-work Americans on numerous public works projects. It was created in 1935.

Celebrating the county's agricultural products would have been quite a normal theme for a school pageant, though it would probably have more likely taken place at a county fair. This pageant contributes to the motif of small-town life.

CHAPTER 28

What happens?

The children pass by the Radley house and into the woods on their way to the school pageant. It is a very dark evening and they scramble about to find their way. Cecil Jacobs jumps out of the bushes and scares both of them out of their wits. They all proceed to the school together, and Scout and Cecil run around to see all the games. It is soon time for the pageant, and the kids get into costume. While Mrs. Merriweather is on stage going on about Maycomb's agriculture, Scout nods off and misses her cue. After being reproached by Mrs. Merriweather, Scout is too embarrassed to face anyone and makes Jem wait to leave until everyone else is already gone. Along with her brother, she heads home, still donning her ham costume, though she realizes once they reach the woods that she has forgotten her shoes.

Jem begins hearing strange noises while they are walking in the pitch-black woods. Thinking it is Cecil Jacobs again, Scout hurls insults into the darkness at her young schoolmate. Jem, however, understands that someone else is lurking about. When they reach the oak tree, their follower attacks them; though Jem yells to Scout to run, she cannot maneuver in her ham costume and falls to ground when something rams into her. Scout can hear Jem fighting, but cannot see with whom. Suddenly, her brother grabs her and begins running, but is yanked back by their attacker. Scout hears more scuffling and then a desperate scream from Jem. Dashing toward her brother, Scout runs into their assailant who violently grabs her before suddenly falling backwards. Scout now hears only the sound of a man panting and manages to see him heading toward the road. She tries to find Jem in the darkness, but comes across the body of a man stinking of alcohol.

Scout hurries to the road and catches a glimpse of the man carrying Jem toward their home. Aunt Alexandra is calling for the doctor, and Atticus is frantically asking after Scout's whereabouts. Learning she is safe, he calls Sheriff Tate. The doctor arrives to examine Jem, and he reassures a worried Scout that her brother will live, though he is unconscious now. Scout enters Jem's room, where Atticus, Alexandra and an unknown man are all gathered. Sheriff Tate arrives and announces that he found Bob Ewell's dead body in the woods. He had been stabbed to death.

Analysis:

This chapter finally reveals the story behind Jem's broken arm, which the narrator referenced in the novel's opening lines. Lee sufficiently foreshadows the attack with Aunt Alexandra's concern for the children before they leave for the school, the dark Halloween night, and Cecil Jacob's prank. Before the danger unfolds, however, Lee creates a charming picture of Maycomb, which gathers for a simple pageant celebrating the town's modest achievements. It is easy to relate to the delight the townspeople would take in seeing children clad in food costumes parade across the stage, even the one who misses her cue. By wedging this happy picture of the small-town South in between the sense of foreboding at the chapter's beginning and the attack at the chapter's end, Lee ingeniously captures the theme of good and evil coexisting.

So far the novel's violence has been abstract. There is no description of how Mayella's father beat her, and Atticus's explanation of Tom Robinson's killing is a secondhand account. But Lee describes this attack in detail and from the first-person perspective of one who experiences it. Though throughout the novel there is a sense of the violence the South's race relations provoke, this is the first time we see its ugly reality in the disturbing form of a man targeting children, a man who is too cowardly to attack their father. Now Jem and Scout are the innocents inflicted by injustice.

It is fitting that Scout is confused about who saves them. Her perception of Boo Radley has always been clouded, first by childhood fear and superstition and later by excessive curiosity. Until she fully humanizes Boo, his presence in the novel and in this pivotal scene is one of a ghost, which befits his name.

Mr. Ewell's attack of innocent children exposes a new depth to his wickedness and prevents any feelings of sympathy or loss over his death. His actions, however, are puzzling as they seem to prove wrong Atticus's conviction that there is good in everyone. Mr. Ewell is evil to the core.

Key takeaways:

When passing the Radley home on their way to the school, Jem and Scout recall their conversation a couple of years earlier about Hot Steams. Jem laughs at the silliness of such notions, a sign that this young man has left childhood mysteries behind him.

The pageant's title is "Ad astra per astera," which is Latin meaning "Through hardships to the stars," or, as Mrs. Merriweather renders it, "From the mud to the stars." It is a hopeful title which signals that, rather than remaining static, Maycomb is indeed on a journey.

CHAPTER 29

What happens?

Sheriff Tate asks Scout what she can remember. Sitting in Atticus's lap she recounts everything she is able to recall. Examining Scout's ham costume, the sheriff discovers a large slice up the side of it where Mr. Ewell must have attempted to stab Scout. Atticus is astonished at the night's events.

Scout resumes her account of the attack and eventually gets to the part where she heard the man panting. The sheriff asks her who the man was, and Scout indicates it was the man now standing in the corner of Jem's room. Noting the man's pale tone, she comes to realize it is Boo Radley who smiles at her.

Analysis:

The final three chapters bring this multi-layered story to a meaningful and dramatic end as we see many of the lessons imparted throughout the narrative come to fruition. Scout gets her wish to meet Boo Radley, and the way their first meeting unfolds is important. Hiding in the corner, Boo remains in the dark, and on the society's periphery, a ghost. But when Scout turns toward him and examines his pale features, her vision of Boo is clear for the first time; she has come out of the society's cloud of misunderstanding and misconceptions about him and is ready to meet the actual person rather than the myth.

CHAPTER 30

What happens?

Atticus introduces Scout to Mr. Arthur Radley. When the doctor returns, everyone goes out to the porch. Atticus begins plotting Jem's defense, but the sheriff questions whether his son actually killed Bob Ewell. Atticus declares that he does not want a cover-up of this crime and is certain Jem could win a self-defense case. But the sheriff, growing somewhat impatient with Atticus, claims there is no need for a cover-up as Bob Ewell accidentally fell on his own knife. Though Atticus objects, Sheriff Tate is unyielding, and he finally succeeds in making Atticus understand that he is not trying to protect Jem, but the shy Boo Radley, whom the sheriff knows is responsible for killing Mr. Ewell. The sheriff also sees poetic justice in the night's events, as Bob Ewell got what was coming to him after the death of Tom Robinson.

Atticus gives in and tells Scout the now official story that Mr. Ewell fell on his knife. With great insight for her young age, Scout explains that saying otherwise would be like killing a mockingbird—the mockingbird is, of course, Boo Radley. Before returning to Jem's side, Atticus thanks Boo.

Analysis:

Atticus's kind but matter-of-fact introduction of Mr. Arthur Radley to Scout confuses his daughter, but also further humanizes Boo in her eyes as she comes to see that there are people who never considered Boo mysterious or scary, only a quiet and perhaps a bit peculiar neighbor. The doctor's nonchalant greeting of Boo reinforces this idea.

Sheriff Tate's determination to protect Boo brings the novel full circle, as the mockingbird metaphor surfaces again. While the sheriff had failed to protect Tom Robinson, he would not fail Boo. Tom's trial showed that Maycomb does not understand justice, and perhaps the sheriff is wary of leaving the fate of someone like Boo, whom most of the town feared for no concrete reason (just as they fear and dislike blacks for no concrete reason), to a jury composed of narrow-minded townspeople. It would be "A sin," according to the Sheriff, a comment that evokes Atticus's admonition that it is a sin to kill a mockingbird.

Atticus hardly has to explain to Scout the reason behind the claim that Mr. Ewell fell on his knife. She understands intuitively and makes the connection to the mockingbird story. It is important to recall that this is not her first experience with a white lie, as she and Atticus had already agreed to keep their reading a secret from Scout's teacher. Her instinctive understanding of the need for this fabrication shows that Scout is learning to see life's nuances and complexities. Finally, the mutual understanding between father and daughter shows that, just like her brother, Scout will grow up to be like Atticus.

CHAPTER 31

What happens?

Scout and Boo head inside to bid Jem goodnight. Scout senses that Boo wants to leave and consents to his request to accompany him home. The two part ways on the Radleys' porch, never to see each other again. Scout remains on the porch, sad that she and Jem never gave Boo anything in return for the kindness he showed them.

Scout takes this opportunity to observe the neighborhood from Boo's perspective and thinks of how he likely saw them playing the "Radley family" game. Atticus's advice comes to Scout's mind as she recalls him saying that you never truly know someone until you walk in his shoes. On her way home, Scout realizes that Jem missed this opportunity to meet the elusive Boo.

At home, Scout finds Atticus reading *The Grey Ghost* in Jem's room. She convinces him to read aloud to her, but she quickly falls asleep. Atticus puts her in bed as she mumbles a poignant part of the book's plot: how the kids in the story chase someone and when they find him, they discover he is quite nice. Atticus remarks that most people are nice once you get to know them, and he returns to wait at Jem's bedside.

Analysis:

Scout's polite, ladylike behavior toward Boo seems to stem less from the prodding and urging to act like a good girl she received from Aunt Alexandra than from the natural inclination to treat another human being with kindness and respect. All of Atticus's lessons and his model behavior have paid off, for Scout understands the connection between civility and goodness.

By pausing to observe the neighborhood from Boo's perspective, Scout puts into practice her father's most important lesson. Seeing Boo as a human being rather than as the town freak or as an object of curiosity, Scout is able to imagine his reaction to seeing them play the "Radley family" game or to never receiving an acknowledgement of his gifts. Empathy for her new acquaintance overcomes the young protagonist.

After a night, and a few years, of being overwhelmed by the realities and unsettling truths of the adult world, Scout retreats back into her childlike self (after all, she is only eight years old) by climbing onto her father's lap and listening to a story. After meeting Boo, she can sleep peacefully as she is now assured of the innate goodness in humans.

Key takeaways:

Jem was Scout's protector and interpreter of the world throughout the story. However, in these final chapters he is silent while she navigates the meeting with Boo and the acceptance of Heck Tate's story alone. Though we are told nothing of what happens to Scout after this night, we know, based on her behavior in these final sections, that she will grow up just fine.

Character List

Jean Louise (Scout) Finch is the novel's protagonist and narrator—the story is told in retrospect from her perspective as an adult. When the novel begins, Scout is a precocious and tomboyish five-year-old. She spends her time playing with her brother, Jem, and neighbor, Dill, occasionally fending off accusations of behaving "Like a girl." Along with the boys, Scout shares a distinct interest in and fear of their reclusive neighbor, Arthur "Boo" Radley, though she is more frightened than the boys by their plan to make contact with him. After a summer of play with Jem and Dill, Scout begins school, which she finds unchallenging. Spontaneous and uncensored, she is prone to schoolyard scraps with boys from her class and to speaking her mind, sometimes at the expense of others' feelings. Without a mother since the age of two, Scout is raised in a predominantly male world of her father and brother, though her caretaker, Calpurnia, and her neighbor, Maudie Atkinson, provide models of feminine behavior, while her Aunt Alexandra attempts to impose on her an extreme version of femininity.

When Atticus's defense of Tom Robinson results in Scout being taunted by neighbors and classmates, she has difficulty curbing her temper. With Atticus's and, at times, Jem's guidance, she manages to better control her emotions, though she still experiences the confusion and impulsive behavior common in a child her age. Tom Robinson's trial heightens Scout's confusion about the world she is growing into as she fails to reconcile the lack of evidence against Tom with the town's determination to have him convicted. Gradually losing her innocence, Scout begins to see the hypocrisy of many of the adults in her community. In contrast to this harsh life lesson, however, is the more hopeful personal evolution she experiences. More evidently than any other of the novel's characters, Scout learns the value of empathy, of trying to understand others by seeing the world from their perspectives.

Jeremy Atticus (Jem) Finch is Scout's elder brother by a four-year age gap. At the novel's beginning, he and Scout are still of ages where they play together—nine years and five years of age respectively. Along with their friend, Dill, Jem and Scout engage in elaborate fantasy play, often acting out scenes from books and, later, imagined scenarios of Boo Radley's life. Jem develops a strong obsession with Boo, and he and Dill concoct schemes to contact their reclusive neighbor. Scout looks up to Jem and cares deeply about him, though she often challenges him in typical scenes of sibling rivalry.

As the novel progresses, Jem hits puberty and begins to prefer his privacy over time spent playing with his little sister. His admiration for Atticus also grows as he matures, and he comes to see his father as a model of gentlemanly, correct behavior. Jem becomes deeply invested in Tom Robinson's trial and is bitterly disillusioned with his hometown when the all-white jury issues a guilty verdict. Lacking his father's mature reason and experience, Jem is unable to discuss the trial as he is overwhelmed with anger whenever the subject arises. At the novel's end, Robert Ewell attacks Jem and breaks his arm in an act of vengeance against the family. Knocked unconscious, Jem misses the opportunity to meet his mysterious neighbor and unexpected savior, Boo Radley.

Atticus Finch is Scout and Jem's widowed father. He is an attorney and serves in the Alabama State Legislature. Atticus is older than most of the children's friends' fathers, and Scout and Jem regret that he is unable to play with them in active or physical ways. Over the course of the novel, however, both children come to appreciate Atticus's principled behavior, gentlemanlike manner, and modesty. Their admiration of him grows especially strong after they witness him shoot a mad dog and come to learn that he is Maycomb's best shot.

In town, Atticus is admired for his intellect, wisdom, fairness and kind behavior. But when Atticus is appointed to represent Tom Robinson and he decides to provide Tom with a real defense, he becomes the object of derision among many residents and of admiration among others, especially the black community. Despite the threats posed to him and his family, Atticus does what he believes is right: to defend a man who was wrongfully accused, regardless of that man's skin color. Atticus's bravery and integrity is quietly and subtly endorsed by several townspeople who respect him, but who themselves are not courageous enough to confront the town's deep-rooted racism in the same outward manner as Atticus does. Throughout the novel, Lee depicts Atticus as the voice of reason in a town where most residents yield uncritically to tradition.

Charles Baker (Dill) Harris is the nephew of Scout and Jem's neighbor, Miss Rachel Haverford, and is six years of age when the novel begins. Throughout the year, he lives with his mother in Mississippi, but spends his summers with his aunt in Maycomb. Dill does not know his father, but concocts wild fantasies about him. Along with Scout and Jem, Dill also fantasizes about Boo Radley and piques his playmates' interest in their puzzling neighbor. Dill proposes to Scout, and the two resolve to marry when they grow up.

At the beginning of the novel's third summer, Dill announces in a letter to Scout and Jem that he will not be visiting Maycomb as his mother has remarried and he will be spending time with them. After only a few weeks, however, he runs away from home and turns up hiding in Jem's room. He remains with his aunt that summer and observes, along with Scout and Jem, Tom Robinson's trial. Dill is particularly distraught at the prosecuting attorney's racist treatment of Tom and leaves the courtroom in tears. Like his friends, Dill experiences the sometimes disorienting aspects of growing up and of learning new truths about a community he thought he knew.

Arthur (Boo) Radley lives two doors away from the Finch family, but no one has seen him for years. As a teenager, he got into trouble while mixing with a dangerous group. His devout and severe father kept Arthur inside the family home until one day, according to town rumors, he stabbed his father in the leg with a pair of scissors. After a few nights in the county jail, where Arthur suffered gravely from the damp, he returned home to resume a life as a recluse. The entire Radley family withdrew from Maycomb social life. Only Arthur's father, and later his elder brother who resided in the family home following the father's death, ever leave the house.

Because of the family's reclusive ways, it became the subject of town gossip. Jem, Scout and Dill develop a growing obsession with "Boo" and give in to their vivid imaginations when pondering what he does all day locked in the family home. They begin acting out scenarios of his life and even attempt to make contact with him. While they treat him as an object of obsession, he begins to make kind gestures toward them, including leaving gifts for them and covering Scout with a blanket when a neighbor's house caught fire in the middle of the night. At the novel's end—the only time Boo actually appears—he rescues Jem and Scout from Robert Ewell's vicious attack. In this final scene, the character of Boo comes to embody one of the novel's primary themes: empathy, or, as Atticus puts it, recognizing that you cannot understand someone until you walk in his shoes.

Calpurnia is the Finches' housekeeper and the children's caretaker. She has worked for years for the extended Finch family at Finch's Landing and began working for Atticus when he married and settled with his wife in Maycomb. She is adored by Atticus and Jem, and while Scout sometimes feels unjustly punished by Calpurnia, she too loves and admires her. Unlike many other blacks in Maycomb County, Calpurnia is literate and aids in teaching Scout to read and write.

In addition to being a surrogate mother to Scout and Jem, Calpurnia also represents a sort of bridge for them to the town's black community. On one occasion, the children accompany her to her church where they are exposed to different practices and customs of worship. Following on this experience, Scout expresses the desire to visit Calpurnia's home. For Atticus, Calpurnia also serves as a link to the town's black community. She accompanies him when he breaks the news to Helen Robinson of her husband's death, and she collects the gifts many black residents leave for Atticus following his ardent defense of Tom. Throughout the novel, the relationship between the Finch family and Calpurnia serves as an ideal of color-blind affection and mutual respect.

Tom Robinson is a married father of four who is falsely accused of raping a white woman, Mayella Ewell. Throughout most of the novel, Tom is known to the reader only as the subject of much town discussion, and he does not appear until the eve of his trial when an angry mob shows up outside the county jail with the intention of lynching him.

Tom speaks for the first time when he takes the stand in his own defense. He comes across as an honest, hard-working man. He stuns the courtroom with his claim that Mayella Ewell made a sexual advance toward him and was beaten by her father when he witnessed her advance. In his defense of Tom, Atticus brings to light a physical ailment he suffers that makes his left arm useless, thus proving that he could not have attacked Mayella in the way she claims. Despite this fact, the all-white male jury finds him guilty of rape. Though Atticus encourages Tom to remain hopeful that the appeal process will exonerate him, Tom quickly loses faith in the idea that justice exists for black men. He attempts an escape from prison, but is shot dead by a guard.

Robert Ewell is the town drunk who is unable to maintain a steady job or to manage the welfare funds he receives. His children are unruly, and there are rumors that he rapes his eldest daughter, Mayella. The Ewell family lives just beyond the town dump near to the Robinsons' home. Ewell is a disgraced figure in Maycomb, but much of the town's white population rally around him when he accuses a black man, Tom Robinson, of raping his daughter, Mayella. On the witness stand during the trial, Ewell displays an arrogant confidence that the all-white jury will believe his version of events. Despite Atticus's best efforts to expose Ewell as a liar, the jury finds in his favor.

Following the trial, the town shuns Ewell, who grows increasingly frustrated and seeks revenge on Atticus. At the novel's end, he attacks Scout and Jem, breaking the latter's arm in the scuffle. Boo Radley intervenes to save the children, and Ewell ends up dead, though it is unclear whether it was Jem or Boo who killed him.

Mayella Violet Ewell is Robert Ewell's eldest child. She accused Tom Robinson of beating and raping her at her home while her father and siblings were out. On the stand during the rape trial, Mayella comes across as an abused young woman and an object of pity. Though Atticus seems close to having her admit her father's guilt, she retreats from issuing such a confession and stubbornly reiterates her false claims that Tom raped her.

Maudie Atkinson lives across the street from the Finch home and is a generous, kind-spirited neighbor who is liberal with the children, allowing them to play in her yard and even take her snow during a freak winter storm, though she fiercely protects her beloved flowers. The children consider her a friend not only because she bakes cakes for them, but because she treats them with respect, unlike many of the adults in the community.

In contrast to Miss Stephanie Crawford, Miss Maudie is not a gossip and is not scared to go against the town's grain. She is one of the few characters who supports Atticus's defense of Tom Robinson, and she is outwardly sympathetic to the plight of blacks in Maycomb. For Scout, Miss Maudie represents a version of southern womanhood she can admire, as Miss Maudie behaves like a lady, but she does not stifle her opinions for the sake of social graces.

Mrs. Henry Lafayette Dubose is the neighborhood lioness. Elderly and widowed, she sits in her wheelchair perched on her porch keeping track of the street's comings and goings. Jem and Scout do everything to avoid her as a walk past her house usually subjects them to bitter tirades about their behavior and dress.

As Tom Robinson's trial nears, Mrs. Dubose launches stinging rants against the children for their father's actions until Jem loses his temper and destroys her camellias. As punishment, he must go to her house each afternoon to read to her for several hours at a time. Within weeks of finishing this task, Jem learns that Mrs. Dubose has passed away and that the real purpose of his visits was to distract her while she was attempting to beat her morphine addiction before dying. Atticus commends Mrs. Dubose for her courage to die "Beholden to nothing and nobody." This lesson in perseverance immediately anticipates the beginning of Tom Robinson's trial where Atticus himself is compelled to show his courage.

Alexandra Hancock is Atticus's sister and Jem and Scout's aunt. She is married to a taciturn, antisocial man, though she herself is outgoing and sociable. She has long disapproved of the way Atticus is raising his children, especially the tomboy Scout. Shortly before Tom Robinson's trial, Aunt Alexandra comes to live with the family. She aims to teach both children about their family heritage and to guide Scout toward more feminine pursuits, a goal which Scout plainly rejects. Aunt Alexandra is initially distressed by Atticus's decision to actively defend Tom Robinson as she is concerned about how his behavior will affect the family's reputation in Maycomb County. But when she learns of Tom's death, she reveals her contempt for the town's deep-seated racism.

John Hale (Uncle Jack) Finch is Atticus's younger brother and the beloved uncle of Scout and Jem. He and Atticus are very similar in their relaxed natures and both are starkly different from their more prim and proper sister, Alexandra. Uncle Jack visits the family at Christmastime and is always a welcome sight to Jem and Scout. He is playful and energetic, but he lacks real experience in parenting and does not always behave fairly toward Scout. However, his openness and willingness to recognize his mistakes endear him to Scout, and she admires his loyalty in not divulging a secret of hers to Atticus.

Heck Tate is Maycomb's sheriff and one of the few adults in the novel who seeks to protect Tom Robinson. Along with Atticus, he tries to shield Robinson from angry mobs intent on hurting him. At the novel's end, Sheriff Tate compels Atticus to go along with the story that Robert Ewell fell on his own knife, as the Sheriff considers unethical the idea of dragging either Jem or the shy Boo Radley through a trial for murder by self-defense.

Judge John Taylor is the presiding judge in Tom Robinson's trial. He seems to understand that Tom is falsely accused and appoints Atticus as his defense attorney in order to ensure that Tom is properly represented. Judge Taylor is rather eccentric and is often depicted as chewing a large cigar or seeming to nod off during the trial.

Helen Robinson is Tom Robinson's wife. After Tom is arrested on rape charges, Helen must care for their children alone. No one is willing to hire her, however, because of the notoriety surrounding the case. Reverend Sykes organizes collections on her behalf at the First Purchase Church. Following Tom's death, Helen is tormented by Robert Ewell, but Link Deas defends her and offers her work.

Miss Stephanie Crawford is the Finch's neighbor. She is a busybody and gossip and is often heard embellishing the town's latest rumors. Though she never directly criticizes Atticus for his role as Tom Robinson's defense attorney, the reader is led to believe that she shares many of the prejudices that prevail among Maycomb's residents.

Grace Merriweather is an outwardly devout member of the Maycomb community and is also known for her love of a drink. Lee satirizes Mrs. Merriweather's professed concern for the far-off Mrunas, presumably an African tribe though it is never specified, by exposing her uncaring and impatient attitude toward her own black servants. Mrs. Merriweather organizes the Halloween pageant at the end of the novel and scolds Scout for missing her cue.

Caroline Fisher is Scout's first-grade teacher. She is new to Maycomb, coming from northern Alabama, and must become acquainted with Maycomb's customs and routines. She is an outsider who resorts to relying on her young students' knowledge of Maycomb in order to make her way in the town.

Walter Cunningham Sr. is a poor farmer who is indebted to Atticus for legal work the latter performed for him. Mr. Cunningham pays Atticus with crops or fruits from his farm. When Tom Robinson is transported to the Maycomb County jail on the eve of his trial, Mr. Cunningham is among the angry mob that confronts Atticus with the intention of lynching Tom. Scout, Jem and Dill intervene and Scout's innocent greeting of Mr. Cunningham serves to defuse the growing tension.

Walter Cunningham Jr. is the son of Mr. Cunningham and one of Scout's schoolmates. On Scout's first day of school, she tries unsuccessfully to explain to the new teacher, Miss Caroline Fisher, why Walter refuses to accept money for lunch. Scout's explanation annoys Miss Fisher, and, out of anger, Scout jumps Walter in the school yard. Jem breaks up the fight and invites Walter home for lunch.

Reverend Sykes is the minister of Maycomb's black Methodist congregation. Scout and Jem meet Reverend Sykes when they accompany Calpurnia to church on a Sunday when Atticus is away from Maycomb. The children are struck by his direct manner in requesting donations from the congregants for the accused Tom Robinson's wife. Scout and Jem meet him again when he accompanies them to the blacks' viewing balcony in the courtroom during Tom Robinson's trial. Jem discusses his certainty that Tom will be cleared of all charges with Reverend Sykes, who is decidedly more skeptical about the potential outcome.

Nathan Radley is Arthur "Boo" Radley's older brother who comes to live at the Radley home following their father's death. His behavior is very similar to his late father's, and he speaks with Scout and Jem only once in the novel, when he is placing cement in the knothole of a tree where Boo had previously left gifts for the children.

Link Deas is Tom Robinson's employer. While Tom is in prison prior to his trial, Mr. Deas refuses to hire Tom's wife, Helen, because he fears showing support of the Robinson family at this sensitive moment. Following Tom's death, however, he gives Helen work and chases off Robert Ewell in his attempts to scare and torment Helen on her way to work. While early on Mr. Deas was critical of Atticus's decision to defend Tom Robinson, he is one of the few minor characters to evolve over the course of the novel toward a more tolerant view of the rights of blacks in the community.

Dolphus Raymond comes from an established Maycomb family, but shocks the entire community by fathering several children with an African-American woman. Outside the courthouse, he socializes with the blacks, holding his ever-present brown bag, which everyone presumes contains whiskey. Scout and Dill later learn that Mr. Raymond has only a bottle of Coca-Cola in the bag but allows it to masquerade as whiskey to put the townspeople at ease. Seeing him as a drunk is the only way they can make sense of his unorthodox lifestyle. The knowledge that he willingly chooses to live with African Americans would upset the community's beliefs and expectations too much. He prefers subterfuge and calm to reality and disturbance.

Braxton Bragg Underwood runs the town newspaper, *The Maycomb Tribune*. While the reader learns from Atticus the well-known truth that he "Despises Negroes," his actions suggest otherwise. When an angry mob appears outside the county jail looking to lynch Tom Robinson on the eve of his trial, Atticus and, unexpectedly, his children fend them off. They later learn that Mr. Bragg was protecting them with a shotgun from the window of his offices above the jail. After Tom's death, Mr. Bragg writes a scathing editorial in his newspaper about the injustice of his trial. Like Mr. Deas, Mr. Bragg is a dynamic minor character whose opinions evolve over the course of the novel.

Horace Gilmer is the prosecuting attorney in Tom Robinson's rape case. He is not from Maycomb, but he shares, at least for expedient purposes, the town's prevailing racism and speaks to Tom using explicitly racist terms.

Themes In The Book

The American South: The American South almost seems like a character in the novel as its particular rules for what is acceptable or unacceptable constitute the motivation behind many of the characters' actions. Aunt Alexandra cannot judge anyone without considering their family history, which, in the South's rigid social order, determined everyone's place. In the early sections of the novel, the narrator, speaking through the eyes of the young Scout, makes sense of everyone in town through a lens of Southern regionalism and gives highly detailed descriptions of Southern womanhood in particular. In the second half of the novel, however, the South's darker side, its ingrained racism, motivates people and exposes the shame of a society that has at its core such irrational hatred.

Prejudice: Though their father instructs Jem and Scout to judge people based on their individual worth, the children come to see that many other people in Maycomb do not think this way. They treat people as groups and categorize them according to race, class, gender and age. Prejudice is the act of holding unreasonable preconceived notions or convictions about a group or race; in its extreme it is an irrational suspicion or hatred of a group.

Prejudice appears in many forms in *To Kill a Mockingbird*. Its most dramatic representation is racism, as we see normally respectable and kind white people convict an innocent black man based on the word of a despicable and sinister man who is believed only because he is white. Maycomb is also prejudiced against Boo Radley, whose behaviors do not conform to expectations and thus qualify him as an outcast or freak. Aunt Alexandra propounds a different sort of prejudice in her blatant classicism while she and others also uphold fixed gender labels. The result of these prejudices is that anyone who does not fit into the town's neatly defined categories is edged out to the society's periphery.

Racial injustice: While the novel deals with the infliction of injustice on innocents in general, it dramatically exposes the racial injustice prominent in the American South. Blacks do not have access to or hope of attaining any real justice. Their fates depend on the will of the whites who operate the legal system and serve on its juries. Despite overwhelming evidence of Tom's innocence, the jury composed of poor white farmers convicts him. Though Atticus believes that the courtroom is "The one place a man ought to get a square deal," he knows the South's unwritten laws, based on deep-seated racism, prohibit fairness. Justice is not blind in Maycomb.

Good and evil: It seems easy to identify the novel's good and bad characters: Atticus is the definitive good man, fair and principled, while Bob Ewell is the bad guy, racist, narrow-minded and wicked. But the way the novel treats the notions of good and evil is actually quite complex. People are generally not at one extreme or the other, but a complex mixture of both good and evil.

Atticus is the exception as he is almost completely good because he understands life's complexities and he actively fights against evil. It is perhaps because of his goodness that Atticus is able to see good in people even when they exhibit bad behavior. He understands that Walter Cunningham Sr. has goodness in him even though he turned up with the angry mob to lynch Tom Robinson. It is this belief in essential goodness that encourages Atticus to fight for what is right and to treat everyone with respect. He tries to introduce this complicated understanding of the coexistence of good and evil within people to his children and encourages them to show empathy and compassion for people before judging them.

Small-town life: Small towns are like humans: complex and contradictory. The positive aspects of small-town life feature prominently in the novel's earlier sections, which show Jem and Scout comforted by a sense of place and belonging and a feeling of safety in this close-knit community where everyone knows everyone else.

As the story progresses, however, the children begin to see negative aspects of small-town life including an absurd social hierarchy based on class and race, an oppressive expectation to accept convention or suffer ostracism, and a strong resistance to change. Despite its many virtues, small-town life is static.

Law vs. social codes: While Maycomb has a courthouse, judges to oversee trials and lawyers to argue cases, the law itself is not absolute. Everyone will acknowledge that an innocent man should go free, but everyone also knows that a black man can never prevail against the word of a white man. In his defense of Tom Robinson, Atticus proves to everyone present that his client is innocent. But the law and its penchant for proof and reasonable doubt had nothing to do with the jury's verdict. Tom Robinson was condemned by Maycomb's rigid social/racial rules which are absolute: whites are superior to blacks. Atticus understands from the outset that the court would be putting Maycomb not Tom Robinson on trial, and he also understands that the law will not prevail.

Coming of age: While the novel idealizes youth, as discussed below, it also represents this life stage as transitory. Youth is a juncture on the path to adulthood. Along this path, young people experience psychological and moral growth. Lee traces the coming of age of both Jem and Scout, exploring adeptly the way they make sense of the adult world they are entering and how they are disoriented by it. Though at different paces and to different degrees, both characters evolve from innocence to an understanding of complex situations.

Class: While race is a predominant theme throughout the novel, class also figures largely. Maycomb is a stratified society divided not only along race lines, but class lines as well. While the Finches represent the upper, educated ranks, farmers, like the Cunninghams, represent the laboring strata, and the lazy Bob Ewell is among the outcasts. While various civil institutions, such as school, bring the various social ranks together, their differences in dress, education and talents are evident. Living civilly in Maycomb requires knowing how to interact with everyone. Atticus is the master of social relations.

Empathy: This is one of the novel's main themes and an essential part of understanding humanity. Atticus repeatedly reminds his children that they cannot fully understand someone until they stand in his or her shoes. When Scout complains about her teacher, Atticus reminds her that her teacher is new to both her job and to Maycomb and may be nervous in her new surroundings. Taking the time to consider the situation, feelings and perspective of another allows one to understand more fully that person's motives. Because of their ingrained prejudices, most people in Maycomb cannot see the plight of the black population or comprehend the injustice inflicted upon Tom Robinson.

Family: Family takes many forms in the novel. For Aunt Alexandra, family is one's lineage and heritage, a marker that denotes one's place in the social hierarchy. Maintaining family honor is of utmost importance to her. For Atticus, family has a looser definition consisting of one's relatives and offspring, but also of those held dear and close, such as Calpurnia, whom Atticus thinks of as a family member. Love is at the basis of Atticus's notion of family. The importance of strong family bonds of love is seen clearly when examining a family that lacks them, such as the Ewells. Love and mutual respect are absent in this household, and all of its members suffer the consequences of this deprivation.

Courage: The theme of courage occurs throughout the novel and is expressed most predominantly through Atticus's actions: his ardent defense of Tom Robinson or his determination to face the angry mob bent on lynching

Tom. For Atticus, these individual examples of courage fall under a more general definition of the notion: to do what is right even when defeat seems certain. He knows the jury will convict Tom Robinson, but Atticus provides Tom with the best defense possible because it is the right thing to do.

Jem and Scout confuse courage with strength and physical ability, but with Atticus's guidance, especially his explanation to them of Mrs. Henry Lafayette Dubose's courageous effort to beat her morphine addiction, the children come to understand that courage means living up to one's moral responsibilities regardless of social consequences. Mr. Underwood bravely stares down Maycomb's racism when he prints his provocative editorial in *The Maycomb Tribune*.

Youth: The fantasy play-world and carefree quality of youth are idealized in the novel. It is a magical moment when children are not only free of the burden and stress of the adult world, but possess a clarity of vision and understanding that is still unpolluted by prejudices that taint adulthood.

About The Book

Harper Lee's *To Kill a Mockingbird* was published in 1960 to both critical acclaim and commercial success. By May 1961, Lee won the Pulitzer Prize for Fiction, and as early as 1962, a film based on the novel, and starring the celebrated actor Gregory Peck as Atticus, was released. In 1963, Peck won the Academy Award for Best Actor for his highly praised depiction of the principled small-town attorney.

Lee drew inspiration for the novel from her own childhood experiences. It is widely accepted among literary scholars that the character of Scout is an autobiographical sketch of Lee herself, who came from the small southern town of Monroeville, Alabama, and was a precocious tomboy prone to schoolyard scraps with her male classmates. Also like Scout, Lee had a brother who was four years her senior, and a father who was a lawyer. Though her mother was not deceased, as Scout's is in the novel, she did suffer from debilitating mental illness and was largely absent from Lee's daily life. Famously, the character of Dill, Scout and Jem's young neighbor, is based on Lee's childhood and lifelong friend, the writer Truman Capote, author of *Breakfast at Tiffany's*. Arthur "Boo" Radley is likewise based on a mysterious figure from Lee's childhood. Capote also depicted a Boo-like character in his first novel *Other Voices, Other Rooms,* which was published in 1948.

Scholars generally consider *To Kill a Mockingbird* as part of a distinct literary context: the post-World War II literature of the American South. Numerous female writers emerged in this literary scene, including Zora Neale Hurston, Flannery O'Connor, Carson McCullers and Eudora Welty. Among the predominant male writers from the South at this time were Truman Capote, William Price Fox, Walker Percy and John Kennedy O'Toole, though O'Toole's works were published posthumously in the 1980s. Most of the writers coming from the American South in this period were deeply influenced by the Civil Rights Movement and incorporated themes of racism, injustice and the conflicts between reason and tradition. Within this literary context, the Southern Gothic style emerged as a prevailing genre with its dominant themes of deeply flawed characters, run-down settings, racism, social marginalization, and sinister happenings that arise from poverty and depravity. Several of the characters and events in *To Kill a Mockingbird* are characteristic of this genre.

Since its original publication in 1960, *To Kill a Mockingbird* has had a long, enduring legacy evident in the fact that it has never been out of print. Lee's rich and layered characterization of small-town life resonates with many who had grown up in a similar setting, and her ability to capture the fantasy world of youth solidified the novel's ongoing appeal to both younger and older audiences. The character of Atticus, with his calm wisdom and understated wit and his role as the voice of reason in a town steeped in tradition, has come to represent the definitive good man: a model, principled citizen and a thoughtful, patient parent. Perhaps more important than all other aspects, Lee's story of humanity contributed to a new understanding of the races when it was first published, and it continues to open readers' minds to the importance of empathy and compassion for others.

Considering Lee's myriad achievements with *To Kill a Mockingbird*, it is surprising that she never completed another novel. According to Rev. Thomas Lane Butts, a friend of Lee's, the author explained her literary silence as follows: "One, I wouldn't go through the pressure and publicity I went through for *To Kill a Mockingbird* for any amount of money. Second, I have said what I wanted to say and will not say it again." Apparently, the extreme attention and accolades in the wake of her novel's success proved too much for Lee, and she opted for a rather Boo-Radley-like response to fame.

About The Author

Nelle Harper Lee was born on April 28, 1926 and raised in the small town of Monroeville, Alabama. The youngest of four children, Lee was a tomboy and gifted intellectually, though she found school dull and unchallenging. Her father, Amasa Coleman Lee, practiced law and was a member of the Alabama State Legislature. Her mother, Frances Cunningham Finch, was incapacitated by mental illness for most of Lee's youth.

Lee began writing as a child and developed intricate stories of intrigue and drama with her childhood friend and neighbor, Truman Capote, who later became a well-known writer known particularly for his novels *Breakfast at Tiffany's* and *In Cold Blood.* In their youth, Lee and Capote were both social outsiders and were drawn to each other due to, among other things, their mutual love of concocting stories. In one of the few interviews Lee has granted since her sudden fame following the publication of *To Kill a Mockingbird*, she explained that in her childhood days her family did not have money or toys and "The result was that we lived in our imagination most of the time. We devised things; we were readers and we could transfer everything we would see on the printed page to the backyard in the form of high drama." No doubt Lee drew from her experiences with the young Capote to depict the elaborate play schemes developed by Scout, Jem and Dill in the early part of the novel.

It is possible that Lee also drew from personal experience for the story's more somber elements, racial injustice and Tom Robinson's rape case. While Lee was young, her father defended two African-American men accused of murdering a white man. Both received the death sentence from an all-white jury. Other cases not directly related to Lee or her family may also have provided the author with a framework for crafting the plot of the rape case. In 1931, the "Scottsboro Boys" case, in which nine black boys were accused of raping two white women, became a national story. The case, which was tried three times, resulted in three guilty verdicts, despite one of the alleged victim's admission that the story was fabricated. Interestingly, one of the defendants was shot to death by a prison guard, not unlike Tom Robinson's fate in Lee's novel. Other parallels between this case and Lee's fictional trial strongly suggest that the author drew on her memories of the Scottsboro Boys to capture the racial tension and high emotion that would surround an interracial rape case in the American South of the 1930s.

Lee remained in Monroeville, Alabama until her college years, when she left to attend Huntingdon College in the state's capital, Montgomery. After only a few semesters, Lee transferred to the University of Alabama in Tuscaloosa where she put her writing skills to work for several university publications. While she enjoyed writing, she chose law for her formal studies and commenced courses toward a postgraduate law degree at the University of Alabama. Soon, however, Lee admitted to her family her aversion for her legal studies. In 1949, at the age of twenty-three, she moved to New York City to pursue a writing career.

Truman Capote may have been responsible for luring Lee to the North. He was already living in New York City by the time she arrived and had published his first novel, *Other Voices, Other Rooms,* the year before. As Capote's fame increased, Lee had to work menial jobs for her first six years in New York. By 1956, however, she had succeeded in finding a literary agent who provided her with a year's allowance to write. At the year's end, Lee had an initial draft of *To Kill a Mockingbird,* which she continued to revise over the next two and half years. When finally published in 1960, the novel debuted to excellent reviews, and Lee won the Pulitzer Prize for Fiction in May 1961.

The fame that accompanied her novel and the subsequent film based on it did not suit Lee's reserved nature. Rather than starting another project on the heels of her success, Lee chose to help Capote research his book *In Cold Blood*, based on the murders of four members of a Kansas family, which was eventually published in 1966. Lee herself never published another novel and has granted very few interviews. In November 2007, Lee received the Presidential Medal of Freedom from President George W. Bush. For most of her adult life, Lee divided her time between New York and Alabama, but she currently resides permanently in Alabama.

Dear Amazon Customer,

Thank you for your purchase. We hope you enjoyed reading the 100-Page Summary of *To Kill a Mocking Bird*. Our team is dedicated to your satisfaction and we want to know if your expectations were met. If for any reason you are unable to leave a favorable rating on Amazon, please email us at info@pylonpublishing.com. We want to know what we need to do to fix the problem and make a better product for all our readers. Your 100% satisfaction is our responsibility.

You can leave us feedback by following the link below or scan the QR code:

Review this book on Amazon

http://tinyurl.com/b57gmmx

Thank you and we look forward to hearing from you.
Sincerely,

Preston
Founder, Pylon Publishing Inc.